JF   09-2420

GEI   Geisert, Bonnie

      Prairie summer

                    $15.00

DATE DUE			

Prairie Summer

Prairie Summer

BONNIE GEISERT

Illustrated by Arthur Geisert

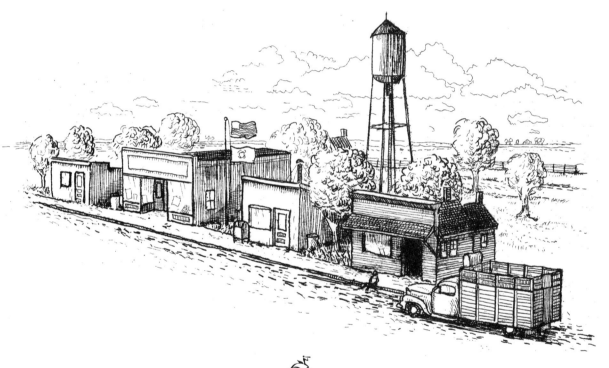

HOUGHTON MIFFLIN COMPANY BOSTON 2002

Walter Lorraine Books

For my Mother — B.G.

Walter Lorraine (wx) Books

Text copyright © 2002 by Bonnie Geisert
Illustrations copyright © 2002 by Arthur Geisert

www.houghtonmifflinbooks.com

09-2420
mifflin
(AmA)
10/09
15.00

Library of Congress Cataloging-In-Publication Data

Geisert, Bonnie.
  Prairie summer / by Bonnie Geisert; illustrated by Arthur Geisert.
    p. cm.
Summary: A young girl demonstrates the maturity gained from her
experiences growing up with three sisters on a farm in South Dakota.
  ISBN 0-618-21293-0
  [1. Farm life—South Dakota—Fiction. 2. Sisters—Fiction. 3. South
Dakota—Fiction.] I. Geisert, Arthur, ill. II. Title.
  PZ7.G2725 Pr 2002
  [Fic]—dc21

                                              2001004176

Printed in the United States of America
VB   10 9 8 7 6 5 4 3 2 1

Prairie Summer

1

The fence didn't stop them. That herd of Montana Black Angus cattle stampeded right through it. They bent the iron posts and snapped the wooden ones off at the ground. Both strands of barbed wire at the top were broken and the woven wire lay on the ground with the bent and broken posts. Now the cattle were in our neighbor Will Hall's pasture.

I saw it happen and could do nothing about it. I was on the Ford

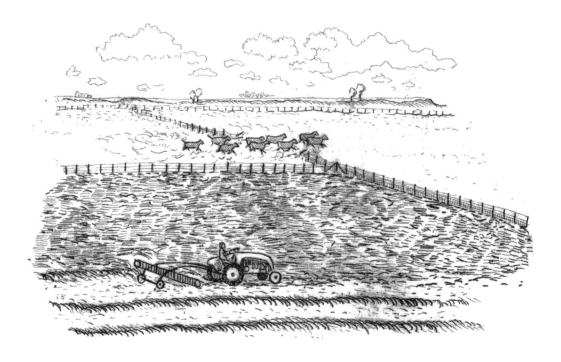

Ferguson tractor a field away pulling a rotary rake, which picks up mowed hay and rolls it into a windrow.

Dad and my thirteen-year-old sister, Carol, who were at home getting the hydraulic farmhand ready for stacking hay, raced to the field in the pickup truck to collect my sister Kim, twelve, who was mowing hay and me, Rachel—ten—to help round up the cattle. We jumped in the back of the truck. Then Dad took the dirt trail that led to the pasture. Kim and I bounced up and down with every bump on the dusty trail. We held on to the truck box for dear life.

The cattle were running around in Will's pasture, mixing with his Herefords and riling them up. Will must have heard the stampede, too. He was driving his pickup truck and honking the horn along his pasture fence line, trying to keep the cattle from running toward it.

The thin Angus cows stopped and stared, their heads high and alert. Dad had bought them in Montana two weeks ago. Since the day they ran off the semitruck into our barnyard in Faulk County, South Dakota, the Angus had spooked easily. In Montana, they were used to open range, where no fences stopped them for miles. The quarter-section pasture where Dad had them was a square of only a quarter-mile on each side.

When Dad got to Will's pasture gate, Kim jumped out and opened it quickly. Dad drove through and waited for Kim to shut it. Then we drove down the opposite side of the pasture from Will, hoping to get around the cattle and run them back toward the barnyard.

Both trucks had worked around the cattle, turning them from their straight-ahead run. The Angus and Herefords started milling around in a circle.

"Get out, girls!" Dad ordered. The three of us were supposed to spread out and keep the cattle from breaking away at the rear while the trucks guarded the sides.

I was scared to death!

One broke and ran in my direction. I was too afraid to stand my ground and wave my arms to turn it back. I ran over toward Kim and the snorting Angus broke past. The rest of the Angus and several Herefords followed.

Dad swung over to us. "Get in!" he snapped.

He raced to the end of the pasture. So did Will. The cattle had gone through one fence. They'd go through another at that speed.

Both trucks bounced along the bumpy pasture on opposite sides of the racing cattle. Both trucks reached the fence line before the herd and turned speeding along the fence, nearly colliding with each other in the middle.

The Angus stopped. We heard their heavy breathing and nervous stamping. Dad waved his arm out the window toward the cattle and yelled, "Turn around, you devils!"

They turned and ran in the other direction. I saw one with a bloody gash across the front of its neck. It must have been one of the lead cows that broke through the fence.

The Angus led the cattle back toward the downed fence. The fatter red white-faced Herefords were slower and trailed behind.

Dad was giving Carol directions. A division between the Angus and Herefords had widened and Dad stopped the truck. Carol got out.

"Rachel, you get out here with Carol," Dad said.

I jumped over the side. Dad sped away after the Angus.

"We're supposed to help Will herd his cattle to his barnyard," Carol said. "We have to make sure they don't go near the broken fence."

"I'd rather work with Will's Herefords than those stupid Montana Angus," I replied.

3

The Herefords were easy to drive to Will's yard. He shut them in his barnyard and scattered some hay from square bales. They were eating and content.

"Thanks, girls!" Will said. "Now jump in and we'll see if we can drive those Angus into your yard."

Carol and I jumped into the back. I was very happy to hear that Will was going to help us. Troubles like this seem so much easier for grown people to deal with. Will drove over the flattened fence like Dad had.

Kim and Dad had gone ahead and opened the corner gate of the pasture that led to the barn. Now they were easing the Angus toward that corner. The Angus had slowed to a trot.

"Maybe they'll get tired of running and slow down," Carol said hopefully. "Dad wants to get them in the barnyard so they won't have so much space to pick up speed and go through the fences."

"Why didn't he think of that right away when they came?" I asked.

"I guess he didn't realize how wild they were," Carol answered.

I stood up to see above the cab and check on what was happening. The herd was trotting along the inner fence line. Kim was on foot behind the herd and Dad was driving the truck along the side. "Carol, look! There's one lowering its head and snorting at Kim!"

"Oh, Lord!" Carol said.

I banged the side of the truck cab. "Hurry, Will! Kim needs help!" I yelled.

Kim waved her arms at the Angus and yelled, "Hi yah!"

"Oh, dear!" I moaned.

The Angus turned around.

Relief flooded my body. *How can she do that?* I wondered.

The herd moved at a slow run and was responding to the guiding of the trucks. Carol and I joined Kim on foot. Dad kept close to the front side of the herd to keep them from running off to the wrong end of the pasture. Will was positioned about halfway, and we ran behind.

There was one tricky spot ahead. Near the barnyard, the fence along one side took a right turn, creating an open area along the creek. Because of the steep banks there, we would have to guard that spot on foot so the cattle wouldn't run past the barnyard gate.

Usually, Dad would feed ground corn to the cattle and call, "Come Boss! Come Boss!" and the cattle would come trotting home from the pasture. These Montana Angus hadn't learned that yet. They were eating pasture grass. Fattening them with corn would come later.

"Carol, I'm scared," I said as we walked to the open spot. "They're so big. There's no way I can stop them if they make a run in my direction."

The three of us made our way carefully behind and around the herd. We moved toward the open spot. The herd was close to the gate. Whether they would go in the gate, run along the fence, turn and run in the opposite direction, or break by us was a guessing game.

"Here, Rachel, Kim! Let's take these sunflower stalks," Carol said. We broke off three dried stalks near the ground. "We can wave them like sticks if they run our way."

We positioned ourselves evenly across the open space. Carol told me to be on the side by the creek. She was in the middle. Kim was on the fence side.

A lead Angus, head high, was leery of the barnyard, but the cattle pushing behind moved through the gate.

Oh, good! I thought, relaxing my body, which had been stiff with fright. That instant, one Angus turned and bolted toward me. I waved my stalk and yelled, but stepped back in fear. My right foot slipped out to the front and suddenly I was flat on my back. I was up in a flash, fearing the Angus would trample me. Carol and Kim had run forward waving their stalks and yelling at the Angus. It turned around and trotted into the barnyard with the last of the cattle. Dad closed the gate behind them.

My pants felt wet and stuck to my behind. A terrible stench was all around me. Before I saw my right shoe covered in slimy green stuff, I realized I had slipped and fallen in a big fresh cow pie. My backside was soaked with manure.

"Oh, Rachel," Carol said with sympathy when she saw me.

Kim wrinkled her nose. "Eww, Rachel! You're a mess!"

I started toward the fence. Carol came, too. She held the strands of barbed wire up so they wouldn't catch my shirt when I climbed over the fence.

I waddled to the house like a baby with a diaper. Tears blurred my sight, then rolled down my cheeks. I couldn't use my dirty hands to wipe them.

That's it! I quit! I told myself on the way to the house. *I'm not doing this anymore!*

2

When I reached the house, I cried out, "Mom? Mama?"

Mom came running outside. Susie was right behind her. Tears were still rolling down my cheeks.

"Oh, honey!" Mom said sympathetically.

Susie was horrified. Her eyes widened, her mouth dropped open, and then she clasped her hand over her nose and mouth.

Mom sent Susie for an old bath towel to wrap around me while she helped me remove my dirty, smelly clothes outside.

In the bathroom, I turned the faucets on wide open and filled the bathtub with hot water. Up to my armpits! For revenge! If Dad's in the house when we're taking baths and he hears the water running longer than he thinks it should, he hollers, "That's enough water!"

His ears really pick up the sound of running water. I'm lucky if the water in the tub is three inches deep before he hollers. Once I had opened the faucet wide up so I wouldn't be able to hear him, hoping to get more water before he hollered. He was at the bathroom door in no time, knocking real loud and yelling, "That's enough water!"

Then he demanded, "Who's in there?"

"Me!" I yelled back.

"No more water, Rachel! You hear?"

"Yeah," I answered resentfully.

Today the deep bath felt good. I soaped my bottom twice, real good. Mom helped me wash my back.

I dried off, put on clean clothes, and told Mom I didn't want to go help with the cattle.

"I'll go check and see if I can help," she said.

I went to my bedroom. Susie went there, too. She played with her panda teddy bear on her side of the bed, and I lay down to read. I read *Little Women* until I fell asleep.

I slept until suppertime.

When I woke up, I felt groggy, but I could hear Dad talking with Mom in the kitchen. "I tell you, Leona, she's practically worthless around the cattle."

My heart sank.

"But Tony, she's only ten," Mom replied. "She's been through a rough afternoon."

Dad kept right on complaining about me. "Carol and Kim turned circles around her when they were her age. She wouldn't have slipped in that manure if she'dve been more alert."

Water filled my eyes. I stared at the ceiling and tried not to blink so tears wouldn't fall. I didn't want my face to show at dinner that I had cried. I had already done that once today and I didn't want to be called a crybaby.

I lay there trying to figure out how I could please Dad. I knew I tried to do the work right, but for some reason I usually goofed up and he'd get mad at me.

Worthless, he had told Mom. He thought I was worthless.

And then I decided if I wasn't going to be appreciated around here, I would go somewhere where I would be appreciated. I wasn't sure where that was, but I made up my mind that I would run away that night.

3

I took the dirt road heading east, the one our family used to get to the east fields. Rarely did anyone else use it, so I doubted that anyone would see me. The night was dark. No moon, but lots of stars.

I had sneaked out of the house after I heard Dad snoring. I was sure everyone was asleep by then. I knew five-year-old Susie would be the hardest one to sneak past. We share a bedroom and she's a light sleeper. Luckily, she didn't wake up when I got out of bed. I heard the sleep breathing of Carol and Kim in their bedroom between Mom and Dad's and Susie's and mine.

I grabbed the pillowcase with a change of shirt, pants, socks, and underpants that I had packed. I also had put in soda crackers, an apple, a carrot, and fresh pea pods, which Mom and I had picked from the garden the day before, and a wad of toilet paper.

I slowly opened the kitchen door to the breezeway, skipped the second step down because it squeaks, carefully turned the latch on the screen door and closed it quietly behind me.

Blackie came running around the corner of the house. The black border collie/German shepherd with white socks and neck is my best friend on the farm. He didn't bark as he approached and he trotted beside me as I walked down the lane.

"Good boy, Blackie," I said, petting the smooth top of his head. I could hardly see his loyal brown eyes in the dark.

The dust muffled our steps in the powdery gray tracks of the dirt road. I would have to be careful not to stumble in the deep ruts

carved by tractor tires last spring when the road was covered with waterholes.

In the sky, the stars were distant miniature lights. I could pick out the Big Dipper and the Little Dipper. The earth was black around us. The black turned to midnight blue where the earth and sky touched. The smell of cut alfalfa filled the air. Cattle lowed in the distant field.

Blackie ran off the road here and there, sniffing.

I smelled a skunk. It had already tangled with something, so I hoped Blackie would keep his distance from it.

When Blackie came back I said, "Stay away from that skunk, Blackie. I've had my fill of stinky stuff for a while."

Blackie ran off again and I heard him rustling around by the fence along the side of the road.

"Hey, Blackie, did you find something good over there?" I called in a low voice. He didn't run over to me like he usually did when I called him.

"Whoo! Whoo!" cut through the still air. Then, light-colored wings flapped softly in front of me. It was an owl, as frightened as I was, flying from its perch on the wooden fence post to a safer perch somewhere else.

I was glad Blackie wasn't barking at anything. It was a quiet night without the wind. Blackie's bark, even away from home, might wake someone.

His white socks, the white tip of his tail, and the white around his neck became easier to see.

It was getting cool, and I hadn't brought a flannel shirt to keep me warm. Although I was only about a mile from home, I was getting a little hungry and tired. I decided to stop by one of the hay bales along the road. *It's a good thing we haven't hauled these bales home yet*, I thought. The bales were from the grass we had cut along the roadsides and baled the week before.

"Here, Blackie! Here, boy!" I called in a low whisper. I saw the white on him bouncing toward me. "Good boy! Let's sit here for a while."

The bale was scratchy on my back, but I was too tired not to lean against it. The warmth from Blackie beside me felt good.

"I didn't pack any food for you, Blackie. Here, try one of these pea pods."

He chewed on it a little bit, then let it lie on the ground.

I shelled my pea pods and ate the peas. Crunchy, sweet, fresh peas. Mom says I eat more raw peas than anybody she knows.

Remembering Mom made me feel sad. She and Susie would be the only ones who would probably miss me. Dad wouldn't miss me.

A shrill "*Yooooowww*" pierced the quiet night. Shivers of fright raced down my neck.

I reached for Blackie. He growled low in his throat.

"That coyote howl isn't far away, Blackie." My voice quivered.

A chorus of yelping followed the howl. "How many are there?" I wondered out loud.

Blackie's ears tensed and his neck hair stiffened. "Shh, Blackie! Stay, boy!"

The next howls were closer.

"They're moving this way," I said in a low voice.

Long, piercing howls followed. Then, more howls came from a side direction. That meant the pack must have been splitting up.

Blackie growled again.

"I don't like this either, Blackie." My heart pounded and my temples felt like a drum was beating from their insides out.

"We're going to have to go home, Blackie," I whispered.

I walked fast, then broke into a run as the howls moved closer. The mile we had covered stretched long in front of us. Blackie ran beside me, panting. I was breathing hard, too.

My side started to ache when we were about halfway home. "I have to stop, Blackie," I gasped. I leaned over, my hand holding my right side where the sharp pain was.

The howls continued from the side and behind.

When the pain let up some, we continued, but slower than before. After a way, Blackie stopped and looked back. He growled. I stopped, too, to give my side a rest. I wondered what chance Blackie and I would have of fighting off a pack of coyotes.

I could see nothing behind me. I heard nothing for a minute either.

Then the howls started again, closer than before. "We'd better run, Blackie!"

Oh please let us make it home before the coyotes catch up to us, I prayed silently.

Finally, I could see the outline of our farm. We had about a hundred yards to go before our lane. The closer we got to home, the better the chance that someone would hear my screams if we were attacked.

"I think . . . we're going . . . to make it, Blackie. I see . . . the . . . lane." I stopped to catch my breath. The howls were closer. Blackie growled and dashed in the direction of the howls.

"Here, boy!" I called. He returned and we continued toward home.

We reached the lane and ran gasping toward the house. The howls had turned to low yelps but seemed very close. We didn't stop until we were a few yards from the house door. My eyes strained through the darkness to the end of the lane. There, I saw the silhouettes of several coyotes milling around as if trying to decide which way to go. They didn't come up the lane. Instead, they decided on the road west and loped away. Their howling had ceased.

"I think we're safe, Blackie." I gave his neck a vigorous rub. I sat down on the grass and Blackie sat beside me. My hands were trembling. In a few minutes, my breathing slowed, the trembling stopped, and the night was still again.

From a high point on the road west, one long howl pierced the darkness. I listened, wishing I knew what the coyote was saying. I stroked Blackie's head for a while. When I quit, he laid it across my lap.

I sat listening for movement in the house, hoping that the piercing howl hadn't woken anyone.

I waited a few minutes before going in. *Please let everyone be asleep*, I prayed. Otherwise, I would have a hard time explaining why I was not in my bed.

4

Luck was with me for a change. I made it back to bed without any-one knowing I was gone. Susie rolled over and mumbled something when I got into bed, but she didn't wake up.

I was still shaking from the coyote scare. I lay awake for a long time. The flight from the coyotes played again and again in my mind. It felt like the same bad nightmare stuck on repeat.

Finally, sleep brought relief.

The noise of pots and pans, dishes, and cupboard doors woke me the next morning. I smelled bacon frying. On the radio Roy Rogers and Dale Evans sang, "Happy trails to you . . . Happy trails to you . . . until we meet again." When they finished, the announcer said, "It's a beautiful sunny morning, May 17, 1954. It's six fifty-five a.m. The temperature is sixty degrees. We'll have sunny skies with a few scattered clouds today and a high temperature near seventy-five degrees."

I heard a meadowlark's song through the window and wished I felt like its cheerful sound. I rolled over to look out the window and discovered that Susie was already gone. She was still enthused about getting up in the mornings.

I rarely got up before being called. Carol and Kim, too. In my half-awake state, I wondered who would rouse Carol, Kim, and me—Mom, Dad, or Susie.

Too soon, I had my answer. "Get up, Rachel!" Susie said, rocking my shoulder back and forth to get my attention. "Dad says it's time to get up."

"Go away!" I snapped. I knew it was a mistake as soon as I said it. She would report it to Dad.

I was aching all over and I felt so tired. Running after the cattle the day before and running away from the coyotes in the night had made me stiff. I trembled a little when I remembered the narrow escape from the coyotes the previous night.

I heard Susie's footsteps head down the hall toward Carol and Kim's room.

"Carol! Kim! Get up! Dad says so!" There was moaning and groaning from their room, but they didn't snap at her.

I got up when I heard Susie's little voice telling Dad, "Rachel said, 'Go away!'" It was funny how exactly she mimicked my words and voice.

I knew what was coming next.

"Rachel! You'd better get up unless you want *me* to come there!" Dad called from his seat at the table by the corner windows.

"I'm up!" I felt tired and cranky, and my answer was borderline sass. A dangerous act.

Every muscle and bone in my body ached when I dressed. It hurt when I squeezed behind Carol and Kim to get to my place behind the table. Susie and I had to sit next to the wall because we were the smallest and the table could be pushed back farther.

I sat with my head propped up by my hand at breakfast. I ate my fried egg, bacon, and toast in slow motion and didn't say anything.

"You must be tired this morning, Rachel," Mom said.

"I am," I replied softly, glad that she didn't know why I was so tired.

"Why should you be tired? You spent most of yesterday on your back," Kim said. Then she laughed.

I saw a smile quiver at the corner of Carol's mouth. Dad smiled.

"That isn't funny!" I snapped.

"It's not nice to make fun of people, Kim," Susie said. "Is it, Mama?"

"That's right, Susie. And Kim knows better." Mom gave Kim a warning look.

I wanted to kick Kim under the table but knew I would get in trouble for it.

"Is there more coffee, Kid?" Dad asked Mom, using the nickname they often called each other.

"Sure, dear!" Mom answered in a soft, warm voice as she rose and went to the stove for the coffeepot.

"Deeear?" Kim questioned, as if to say, *Did you hear that?* She nudged Carol with her elbow.

Carol moved her eyebrows in a "hubba, hubba" manner.

Mom poured Dad's coffee. Her long dark hair was pulled behind her ears and held by bobby pins. Dad looked up at her with mushy eyes. She bent over and kissed his cheek.

It was embarrassing.

"Daddy loves Mama!" Susie sang out.

"And Mama loves Daddy," Mom said.

Oh, good grief, I thought.

Kim and Carol rolled their eyes at each other.

"Well, I guess we'd better get down to business," Dad said after taking a careful sip of his fresh coffee. "Carol, you'll help me fix that darn fence the cows broke all to pieces. Kim, you'll finish mowing the field you started yesterday. And Rachel, you'll finish raking the field you were in."

None of us whooped for joy.

"What am I going to do?" Susie asked.

"Your mama is going to Faulkton this morning. I imagine she'll want you to go with her. Right, Kid?"

"Right. Susie's going with me."

"Oh, goody!" Susie clapped her hands.

"What's Mom going to Faulkton for?" Kim asked.

A look passed between Mom and Dad.

"She has to pick up some salt blocks for the cattle," Dad said.

There was something more. You could tell by the hesitation when he answered. Whatever it was, we would have to wait to find out. His voice had that end-of-discussion tone.

Dad drove me out to the Ford tractor and rake. Neither of us spoke. Before I started raking, he poured the gas from a five-gallon can into the tractor's gas tank.

I greased the rake. The grease gun was heavy in my hand, so I knew it was full. I placed the gun nozzle over a grease zerk on the rake bar and pumped the lever handle up and down. Soon I felt the grease pushing through the thin tube and into the zerk. I pumped the gun until a glob of grease oozed around the edge of the zerk, signaling that it would accept no more grease. I did the same with all the zerks on the rake.

The rake was ready for work. The tractor was ready for work. I was there because I had to be.

Dad walked to a windrow and picked up a handful of hay, fingering it. "She's a little damp this morning, but by this afternoon she should be ready to stack." He wasn't really talking to me. Just talking out loud.

I didn't answer. I didn't feel like talking.

He dropped the hay on the windrow and said, "If we're still fixing fence when you get done, drive to the corner of the field and walk over to help us."

I nodded my head slightly. He didn't see.

"Did you hear?" he asked.

"Yes, I heard." My tone was impatient.

"Well, then . . ." he said and dropped the subject. He got into the pickup and drove back to the farm to load the fencing materials.

During the monotonous trips around the field, I relived the cattle adventure of the day before and the night's coyote scare. This morning the cattle had settled down in the barnyard with ground corn to eat. The coyotes were probably in their dens, wherever those were, for the day.

I finished raking late that morning and then drove to the corner of the field closest to the broken fence. I wasn't near a gate, so I climbed over the fence by a wooden post. We always climbed over by a wooden post. Dad's orders. The steel posts don't support the wire as well as the wooden posts.

"A loose wire is just inviting a cow to push it out and eat the grass on the other side. The more the cows push it out, the more wires they tear loose," Dad would lecture after catching one of us climbing by a steel post.

Dad was digging the hole for the last wooden post. He is the only one strong enough. He was turning the wooden T handle of the post-hole digger around and around. Inch by inch, the digger lowered into the hole. When the digger's curved metal blades were full of dirt, he pulled the digger out of the hole and tapped it on the ground nearby to empty it.

"Got that field raked, did you?" he asked, stopping briefly to look at me.

"Yup," I answered, waiting for a reprimand for something.

Instead, he lowered the digger into the hole again. The metal blades scraped against a rock. If it was a small rock, it would jiggle free with a few grunts and turns of the handle.

It wasn't.

"Reach me that crowbar," he said to me.

I held the curved end of the metal bar out to him. Dad pulled up the digger. The small amount of dirt in it slid out. With the crowbar, he pushed against the rock and dug around in the hole, trying to loosen the rock. Beads of sweat dropped from the end of his nose. He took a swipe across his face with the top of his arm, using his sleeve to wipe the dripping sweat.

I stayed nearby to fetch tools and be the gopher. It was funny the first time I heard Dad tell Susie she was going to be the gopher.

"Gopher!" she had exclaimed. "I don't want to be a gopher!"

"You're always my gopher when you help me, Susie," he said. "You go fer this and you go fer that for me."

"Oh, you silly man! You mean go *for*!"

"That's what I said—go fer," he teased.

"No, *go for*," she insisted.

"Oh, okay. Go for," he said and the game stopped.

For some reason, he never had time to tease me.

"This is a good-sized rock in here," Dad grunted. He had been pushing and pulling with the crowbar to loosen it. He laid the crowbar on the ground and reached in the hole with his arm.

"That sucker should come out," he said. He reached farther, digging the dirt away from the rock with his hand.

"I'll need the spade to make this hole wider," he said. That was my gopher cue.

You don't saunter when you're a gopher for Dad. I dashed for the spade, which lay a few feet away, and handed it to him. He was standing, ready for it, and grabbed it out of my hand. He dug the hole wider. This was going to be a time-consuming hole. Some holes take a long time to dig, depending on how many rocks are in the hole or how dry and hard the clay-like soil is. Sometimes we have to put water in the holes if the soil is too hard to dig. We wait until the water has soaked into the soil before digging deeper. Sometimes it's a long wait.

I ambled toward Carol, who was tamping the reddish brown soil around the last wooden post being replaced. Although it was hot, Carol had a long-sleeved shirt over her blouse to keep the sun off her arms. She wore a wide-brimmed straw hat to shade her face, and she had canvas work gloves to protect her hands and long fingernails.

She lifted a long, solid steel bar with one end slightly broadened and then dropped that end again and again to pound the soil in the hole around the post. This held the post tight in the hole and kept it straight. The excess dirt from the hole was packed and mounded around the post, giving extra security.

The smell of oil on the posts reminded me of the Miranda Hardware and Lumber Company, where they had lots of posts in

22

piles. Miranda is a small town about eight miles south. Philip Finson and his wife owned the lumberyard.

"Carol, is it true that Philip Finson is a millionaire and owns a solid block of buildings in Chicago?" I asked.

"That's what people say," she answered, pressing her foot on the soil to pack it one last time against the post.

"Why do they wait in the dark in their store until someone comes in?" I asked.

"They save money on their electric bill, I guess," she answered.

The last time I was there with Dad, it was dark when we entered the hardware store. Philip got up from his chair and pulled the string to turn on the bare light bulb hanging overhead. The bulb swung slowly back and forth. Shadows from tools and metal buckets on the shelves and items around the room swayed back and forth.

Dad asked for some three-quarter-inch nuts and bolts, and Philip walked down one of the aisles. He pulled the string of the light in that aisle. After getting the nuts and bolts, he pulled the string and turned off the light. He put the nuts and bolts in a thick brown paper bag and told Dad how much he owed. Philip pressed a long curved button on a large brass cash register and a drawer at the bottom came out at him. A bell rang at the same time.

When we left, he pulled the string on the light.

"They say his wife has only one dress," Carol said.

"One dress!" I exclaimed. "She had a dress on about a month ago when I was along with Dad and she was tending the store. It was pink with blue flowers."

"It could be a story to exaggerate how frugal they are," Carol said.

"Frugal?" I asked. Carol often used big words. She was considered brainy.

"Frugal means saving your money and spending it mainly for necessities."

She packed the dirt around the post one more time with her shoe. "There, this one is done," she said.

We walked over to Dad, who was shoving dirt with his boot into the post hole while holding the post up straight. A large pink granite rock coated with dirt lay on the ground near the post.

"I'll finish this one. You can drive those steel posts into the ground," Dad told Carol.

"Rachel, will you get the driver for me?" Carol asked.

I ran to get the driver, which was lying by a steel post about fifty feet away. The hollow steel cylinder with one closed end was heavy.

The steel posts were laid out earlier by Carol and Dad. Dad removed the posts from the pickup while Carol slowly drove along the fence line. Dad measured the distance between posts by his stride. He walked eight paces then laid down a steel post, eight paces, another steel post, eight paces, another post. Then he started the posts into the ground so it was easier for Carol to finish pounding them in.

Carol placed the hollow driver over a steel post. She raised and then with force lowered the driver until the closed end banged the top of the post and drove it into the ground. She repeated the up-and-down thrusts until the fin-like flange about eighteen inches from the bottom of the post disappeared into the ground. It took her eight thrusts to pound this post far enough into the ground. The next one took seven. It would probably have taken Dad only two or three.

Carol continued down the line of posts. There were four steel posts for every wooden one. When two were left, Carol ran into a problem. The post hit a rock and wouldn't budge.

Dad came to her rescue after he finished packing the dirt around the wooden post. He pushed back and forth on the steel post to loosen it and then pulled it out of the ground. He moved it over a few inches and started driving it into the ground.

A streak of dust on the gravel road a mile away caught my eye. I elbowed Carol when I recognized our car. "Mom's coming home from Faulkton," I said softly so Dad wouldn't hear. "What do you think was such a secret about the trip?"

"I don't know," Carol said. "But you know how we'll find out don't you?" she added in a sly whisper.

I knew what she meant. It always worked.

Dad headed for the last post and drove it into the ground.

"Time to break for lunch," he said. "We'll put up the wire this afternoon."

That was good news to me. My stomach had been growling for half an hour.

"Mom should be back from Faulkton by now, too," he added.

Neither of us mentioned that we had seen her return.

5

"Psst, Susie! Come here!" I whispered, beckoning with my finger.

Carol, Kim, and I had gathered in their bedroom while Dad was washing up in the bathroom and Mom was busy making lunch in the kitchen.

"Come in here," I coaxed, backing into the bedroom. She followed

me into the hallway and then into the bedroom. "We want to ask you something."

"What?" she asked.

I closed the door, careful not to catch the latch so a click wouldn't be heard. It's surprising how loud a door shut in stealth could be in this house.

"Where else did Mom go in Faulkton besides the feed store?" Carol asked in a low voice.

"The doctor's office," Susie answered matter-of-factly.

"The doctor's office?" the three of us asked nearly in unison.

"Uh huh." Susie nodded her head.

"Was she sick?" Kim asked.

"I don't think so. She didn't act sick," Susie said.

"I hope she isn't sick," Carol said soberly.

"She doesn't look sick," Kim said.

"Why would she go to the doctor's office if she isn't sick?" I asked.

Suddenly, the door swung open and Dad's big frame filled the doorway. "What's going on in here?" he asked.

"They want to know where Mama went in Faulkton," Susie blurted out.

"And what did you tell them?"

"The doctor's office," she said with a shrug of her shoulders. "That's where we went."

"Is . . . Mom sick?" Carol asked.

"Hey, Kid, can you come here a minute?" Dad called toward the kitchen.

"Where's here?" she called back.

"Carol and Kim's bedroom."

We heard Mom's footsteps nearing. "What's everyone doing in here?" she said, laughing.

"It seems the girls asked Susie where you went in Faulkton. And now they are worried that you might be sick," Dad told her.

She gave him a sheepish smile. "I guess this is as good a time as any to tell them. Do you agree?"

"Sure," he said.

"We are expecting a baby, girls!" Mom said.

"A baby!" Kim exclaimed.

"Another baby?" Carol asked. "We already have four kids."

"How embarrassing!" I grumbled. "What will our friends think?"

The room was silent. Mom's face faded and Dad looked angry.

"*I'd* like to have a baby," Susie said.

"Just wait until you have to help take care of it," Kim told her.

"That's enough!" Dad snapped. "What kind of girls are you anyway?"

"Obviously, they're the kind that don't want another baby in the family," Mom said. She looked sad as she left the room.

"You'd better find a way to make this right!" Dad said, shaking his finger angrily at us. "Come on, Susie, let's go help Mama with lunch."

Kim waited a few seconds after they were gone. Then she said in disgust, her voice low, "This means they *did it* again."

"I'm not telling any of my friends there's going to be another baby," I said.

"There isn't anything we can do about it," Carol said. "We hurt Mom's feelings and we have to apologize."

"I'm sorry we made Mom sad," I said. "But I still don't like the idea of another baby in the family."

We sat in silence for a minute. Then the door was pushed open. This time Susie stood there, her face barely even with the doorknob. "Lunch is ready," she announced, then added indignantly, "you big bad girls!"

"Watch it, punk," Kim snapped back as Susie left.

"The first thing we do is apologize to Mom," Carol said.

We traipsed out of the room, Carol in the lead, me last. Mom was at the sink, her back to us.

"I'm sorry, Mom, that I wasn't very nice about the baby," Carol said.

"Me, too," Kim said.

"I'm sorry I made you sad," I said.

Mom nodded her head. It was a forgiving nod, but she didn't turn to face us. She lifted her apron to her face, but it didn't quite reach, so she had to lower her face to touch the apron to her eyes.

We took our places at the table. Dad looked at us in disgust.

It was a quiet meal until Susie asked, "Do you feel better, Mama?"

"Yes, Susie."

"When do we get the new baby?"

"You should have a new brother or sister in September," Mom replied.

Susie took a bite of her mashed potatoes in contemplation, then said, "I want a sister to play house with me."

"Oh, you do?" Mom replied.

"Yeah." Then a puzzled look crossed Susie's face.

"How does the baby get to be a brother or sister?"

"Oh, it just happens," Mom said smiling.

I was glad she didn't want to explain the details of the birds and bees to Susie right then.

I looked at Mom. Her apron was noticeably tighter and her stomach curved out. Most of the time around home she wore loose shirts over slacks, which had hidden her growing middle.

It was a somber meal. When Dad finished, he placed his silverware on his plate and pushed it away from him so he could put his arms on the table while he drank his coffee. He looked out the window, where he could see any occasional traffic on the county road a mile away.

When his coffee was finished, he summarized the afternoon's work. "Kim will finish mowing the field she's in. Carol and Rachel will help me put up the fence wire. If that goes okay, we still may be able to start that south field haystack."

No one moved.

"Well, this isn't getting it done," he said, pushing his chair back and rising. "Thanks for lunch, Kid.

"Susie, are you gonna help your mom at home?"

"Yup!" she answered with a big nod.

"I have some ice water and iced tea ready, Kid," Mom said. She got the water and tea from the refrigerator and handed a half-gallon jar of tea to Carol and the water to me. The ice clinked against the sides of the glass jar. Two-pieced canning lids at the top prevented any leaking.

On the way to the field, Kim rode in the back of the pickup because she would get out first. I sat between Carol and Dad in the front, holding the cold water jar between my knees. The jar started to sweat and my jeans felt damp. I had to lean toward Carol so Dad's big elbow didn't hit me in the head.

At the fence, Dad took a sack of wire fasteners, a sack of staples, a pair of pliers, and a hammer out of the pickup bed and handed them to Carol and me. Then he took out some baling wire.

Carol helped Dad lift the woven wire against the fence posts. I handed Dad the wire fasteners, which attached the wire to the steel posts, and the staples, which nailed the wire to the wooden posts. Dad secured the wire with two fasteners or two staples at the top and to every other wire that crossed the post until he got to the second wire from the bottom, where both wires were again secured.

30

This gave the wire a tight fit and discouraged cattle from poking their mouths through the fence to get the greener grass on the other side.

The woven wire repair went along without a hitch.

The difficult part of fence mending is patching and stretching the broken barbed wire. The sharp barbs, sticking out from the wire every five inches, are nasty. They catch your clothes and cut your skin. I used to think barbed wire was barbed wire until I saw umpteen different kinds of it on display in a museum.

Putting two strands above the woven wire is standard. That keeps cows from reaching over the fence to eat whatever they think is better over there.

Dad retrieved his leather gloves from under the driver's seat. He put them on, then lifted a wire stretcher and roll of barbed wire from the back.

"Rachel, bring the wire cutter," Dad ordered.

I ran to get it. *Why doesn't he ever say "please"?* I wondered.

By the fence he found the loose ends of the barbed wire and pulled them together. He cut a small section of wire from the roll and coiled it tightly around one end. Then he attached one end of the wire stretcher on each of the pieces.

The stretcher had a lever handle on it, and with each back-and-forth pull, the wire was pulled together from each side. The tighter the wires became, the harder the handle was to work.

There wasn't anything Carol and I could do to help until the wire was stretched and joined, so we stood back a little from the fence and watched. Dad would need his pliers, and they were within handy reach at his side in his overalls loop.

"This can take one more notch," Dad said.

Suddenly, a twang vibrated along the fence, and an angry curse slipped from Dad's lips.

I felt a sharp sting on my left cheek below my eye. The sting turned to pain, and blood was dripping on my shirt. I felt my cheek. Blood filled my hand.

"Carol," I cried frantically.

"Dad!" she screamed after she looked at me.

When he saw my bloody face, Dad dropped his tools. "Oh, Lord," he said. He took his red handkerchief from his back pocket as he rushed to us. He pressed the handkerchief to my cheek. "Hold this against your cheek. Let's see if it will stop bleeding."

"I feel weak," I said.

"Lie down on the ground for a minute, then," Dad said.

Carol helped me down. I was shaking with fright. I lay there with my eyes closed.

"You should have been further back from the fence," Dad said.

Carol said nothing.

Had I not been on the ground, I would have been tempted to say, "You should know when the wire is tight enough!"

"Let me see if the bleeding has stopped," Carol said. I removed my bloody hand so she could lift the handkerchief.

"The bleeding is slowing," she reported.

"Carol, you better take Rachel home and have your mother take care of that cut," Dad said. "I'll stay here and see if I can finish this fence."

"Can you get up, Rachel?" Carol asked.

"I think so." I started to get up.

"Here, let me help you," she said, putting her arm under my armpit to give me support. We walked to the pickup.

"I'd better keep that jar of water with me," Dad said and took it out of the pickup. I heard him unscrew the lid and gulp down some water. I knew without looking that he'd put it on the shady side of the nearest wooden post.

Carol drove home slowly, but the wheels seemed to hit every badger and prairie dog hole in the field. I was afraid the jostling would start the bleeding again.

When Mom saw me she gasped. "What happened?"

"The barbed wire snapped when Dad stretched it," Carol replied.

"For heaven's sake!" Mom exclaimed.

"It hurts!" I moaned, still holding the handkerchief to my cheek.

Mom helped me to a chair by the kitchen sink. She wanted the bright light coming in the kitchen window. She took a clean cloth torn from an old dishtowel and washed the cut. "I don't think this is deep enough for stitches," she said, "but it's a long cut."

"Ow!" I bawled as she dabbed the wet towel along the cut.

"Unfortunately, it's going to hurt, and it will be sore for a day or two.

"You may not know it now, young lady, but you are a lucky girl.

33

An inch higher and it would have been your eye. It makes me shudder to think about it."

"Will I have another scar?" I already had scars above the outer corner of each eye.

"Time will tell," Mom answered. "Prepare yourself. This will sting."

She took a small bottle of reddish liquid that said "Mercurochrome" on it. She unscrewed the cap and pulled out the thin glass tube attached to it. The tube was wet with red liquid. "Hold still," she warned and then dabbed the tube along my cut.

I stifled an "Ow!" and tensed my body against the pain.

"I know, it stings," Mom purred sympathetically.

She dipped the tube into the bottle and continued gently dabbing along the cut.

"Almost done," she said, and then, "Good girl!" as she came to the end. "Now hold this piece of gauze lightly over the cut and I'll tape it down. That'll keep the dirt out." She snipped pieces of white cloth tape and pressed them gently over the gauze.

"There. That should take care of it for now. I want you to take it easy for the rest of the day."

I hoped she had in mind lying around and reading. I wanted to lose myself in the world of Jo, Meg, Beth, and Amy March in *Little Women*.

"Carol, you can go back to help your dad with the fencing. You be careful. And tell your dad to be careful," Mom said.

"I'll need all the help I can get raising five kids," she added to herself after Carol went out the door.

Then I remembered the baby and how nasty I'd been. I remembered making Mom cry with my mean words. *That's why this happened to me*, I thought.

"Mom, I'm sorry for what I said about the baby. I deserve this cut.

It's my punishment for being mean to you. I deserve this."

"Oh, no, Rachel, don't think that. You were merely in the wrong place at the wrong time. It was an accident and that's all."

"Is that the way Dad will look at it?"

"What do you mean?"

"I bet he thinks it's my punishment."

"No, Rachel, your dad wouldn't think that."

"Well, he's always blaming me for stuff."

6

My cut cheek gave me a break from work the next day. I heard Mom tell Dad that night that she thought another day of rest would be good for me.

"Well, I'm not so sure, Kid," he said. "We don't want these girls to get soft."

"One day off isn't going to make her soft," Mom said, laughing.

"She's already soft," he replied.

"I think she's tougher than you give her credit for," Mom said in my defense.

There was no reply.

What can I do to please him? I wondered after hearing that. *I do everything he tells me to and I do it the best I can. Most of the things I just don't like doing.*

I know one thing—when I grow up, I am not going to marry a farmer!

Around noon, I heard Mom in the kitchen clanging pots and pans as she got them out of drawers. I closed *Little Women* and went to the kitchen. Mom was in the cooking and cupboard part of the kitchen, which was separated from the dining section by a glass-block bar held in place by a maple wood frame.

"Can I help with anything, Mom?"

"Sure. You can peel these potatoes for me. I've already washed them."

Several large potatoes were waiting in the sink. I got a paring

knife out of the silverware drawer and started peeling the potatoes. I placed each one in the cooking pot Mom had ready and filled the pot with enough water to cover the potatoes the way I had seen Mom do many times.

"Are we having boiled potatoes or mashed?" I asked.

"Mashed, if I have time."

"Good. That's my favorite."

Mom placed the potato pot on a rear burner of the electric stove.

"Do you see them coming home yet?" she asked.

I looked out the window. At first, I thought my eyes were playing a trick on me when I saw the Ford tractor veer and disappear into the steep ditch by the creek bend.

"The tractor's in the ditch!" I yelled.

"What?" Mom leaned over the sink to look out the window for herself. Suddenly, the tractor was up on the bank between the ditch and the creek, headed for the creek.

"Susie!" we shouted when we could barely see a driver.

"Come on, Rachel, we'll take the car down."

We dashed to the garage, Mom pleading softly, "Please, God, not in the creek. Not in the creek."

We pushed up the garage door as fast as we could and got in the car. Mom backed out and sped down the lane.

"I see the tractor!" I pointed out the window. "It's still on the bank."

"Just stay there, Susie," Mom wished aloud.

The tractor stopped. "I hope she knows how to turn it off," I said.

When we were close to where Susie was, Mom stopped the car on the road. The tractor motor was still idling. Susie was standing on the clutch pedal with both feet to hold it down.

"Stay just like that, Susie," Mom called to her. "I'll come and help you."

We ran down the steep ditch, up the bank, and toward the tractor. Mom stepped up on the back hitching bar, stretched over the seat, and turned off the ignition. She stepped down from the tractor and laid her head on her arms, resting them on the back of the tractor seat for a second. Her face was pale.

"Hey, can I get down now?" Susie asked. Her voice was much too calm for the close call she had just had. The bank dropped abruptly to the creek about ten feet beyond the tractor, and the creek was deep there.

"Yeah, Susie. The tractor's off and you can get down," I said, my voice quivering. The cut on my face was aching.

Susie jumped down, and the clutch pedal sprang up with a clunk.

Mom was still leaning her head on the tractor seat. "Mom? You okay?" I asked.

"I will be in a minute," she said, lifting her head. Her hand went to the side of her curved stomach as though it bothered her.

Susie came over to her. "Mama?" she questioned.

"Susie! My baby! That was a close call!" Mom pulled her to her, leaned down to kiss the top of her hair, and gave her a lingering hug.

When Mom released her she asked, "Why were you driving that tractor, Susie?"

"I asked Daddy if I could. He showed me how and then told me to drive it home," she said proudly.

Mom patted Susie's cheek, then shook her head and looked away. Anger showed in her hazel eyes. The warm breeze blew her dark shoulder-length hair away from her face.

You can bet she's mad at Dad for letting Susie drive that tractor! I thought. Most of us didn't drive the Ford until we were six, bigger than Susie, and strong enough to hold the clutch down with one foot.

"I'll drive the tractor home, Mom," I offered. There was an approach to the road a few hundred feet ahead, and I would be able to avoid the creek with a sharp turn.

"No, Rachel, we'll leave it right here so your dad can see it and get some idea of what occurred. Let *his* heart race when he imagines what could have happened!"

7

Mom was mad at Dad. She didn't talk much and had a long face when he was around. She answered his questions with "yes," "no," or "I don't know." Meals were hurried. That night she mended and ironed clothes in the kitchen rather than in the living room as usual, where Dad listened to the radio or read his newspaper and farming magazines.

The next day, we stacked hay without Mom. Dad said she wasn't helping because she was expecting, but we girls had it figured out that she was too mad at Dad to help. After all, he often teased that she was his "best pitchfork man."

We stacked the alfalfa that I had finished raking two days before. Dad was worried about losing the leaves if the hay dried too long before stacking it. The leaves drop off when jostled if the hay is too dry. On the other hand, the hay can't be too wet or it could rot in the stack or catch fire from spontaneous combustion.

We'd had a couple of wasted days fixing the fence broken by the wild Angus, who seemed to be settling down. They didn't spook as much when someone set foot in the yard to feed them. They even headed toward the feed bunks while the feed was being scooped from the wagon.

That morning when Dad assigned feeding the Angus to me, fear raced through every cell in my body. My face must have gone pale, because he then added Kim to that chore.

Kim had little fear around the animals. She climbed over the wooden gate to the yard and headed to the feed wagon like she was boss and they'd better not mess with her. I climbed to the top of the gate and stayed there.

The Angus trotted toward the perimeter of the yard but started back to the bunks when Kim tossed scoops of the yellow powdered corn from the wagon into the bunks. The bunks winged out from both sides of the metal feed wagon like long narrow food trays just the right height for a cow's mouth.

When the first scoops of grain hit the bunk, the cattle pushed in around the bunk, vying for good feeding positions. They were in constant motion. Kim couldn't toss the grain with the cattle there because it would land on their heads and be wasted. She had to lower the scoop shovel into the bunk and then push the corn along the bunks to the end, shooing the cattle back so she could get through.

"This would be easier if you would help!" she shouted to me. At the sound of her voice, several cattle near her backed nervously away. They were packed in so tightly, that's the only direction they could move.

"I'm afraid of them!" I hollered back.

"They're eating! They won't pay any attention if you walk over here."

Then I remembered my cut, which had a healthy scab and was healing more quickly than I liked. "What about my cut?"

"Ha!" she mocked, then threatened, "You'd better help or I'm gonna tell Dad!"

Great! I thought. *One more thing to get him mad at me.*

"You'd better help or I'm gonna tell Dad," I mimicked, wrinkling my nose at her.

But I didn't like the idea of more contention with Dad, so I waited until the cattle pushed back to the bunk to feed, then

41

carefully walked toward the wagon, making sure only rear ends were facing me. That's not the prettiest sight in the world. Cattle don't use toilet paper.

I made it to the wagon and jumped up on one of the rubber tires. A little courage crept into me, and I was curious to see what would happen if I kicked the cow nearest the wagon in the side rump. Nothing. I kicked again. Hurting it was not the farthest thought from my mind, since these cows had caused me so much physical and mental misery.

"*What* are you doing?" Kim snapped.

That spooked them. Half of the cows backed out and ran away. The rest kept shoving the coarse powdered yellow meal into their mouths with their tongues, mixing it with saliva, and grinding it a

bit with their molars before swallowing it.

"Do you want to scoop or push the feed down the bunks?" Kim asked.

"I'll scoop," I said, glad she gave me a choice.

After I climbed into the wagon, the cows came slowly back to eat. I lifted the scoops of grain over the wagon side and set them in the bunk. Then Kim pushed the grain along the bunk.

"Twenty scoops in each bunk, Dad said. But you'd better make it twenty-five. Your scoops are smaller than mine," she said.

By the time we'd filled both bunks, the cattle all had feeding spots and were settled down. When we were done, I walked to the gate beside Kim on the side away from the cows. A couple of cows lifted their heads and watched us. The rest paid no attention. I could hear their tongues scraping the ground corn all the way to the gate. It sounded like sandpaper on rough boards.

After feeding the cattle, Kim and I walked to the field to help Dad and Carol put up a new haystack frame. We crossed the creek on the rocks that had been piled up to form a dam. Little minnows, like small shiny ribbons, darted and twisted in all directions in the clear, shallow water.

When we got to the field, three sides of the frame were up. This year Dad was using orange-painted metal bar gates instead of the heavy wooden gates for the frames. Each gate was fifteen feet long and anchored with baling wire to steel posts, which can be removed from the ground. We wired two fifteen-foot gates at each end and four along the sides, and the frame was ready.

Dad picked up a handful of hay from the nearest windrow and felt to see if the morning dew had dried.

"It's haystacking time!" he declared.

I didn't share his excitement. Carol and Kim didn't give a cheer either. It was going to be a long, hot day in the sun, which wouldn't set until nine o'clock that night.

With purpose in his stride, Dad headed for the tractor with the hydraulic farmhand—a large metal framework bolted to the tractor at the hitching bar and at the sides of the chassis. He turned down the canvas-padded seat, which had been flipped upside down in case it rained, climbed into the seat, and pushed the starter. He drove the tractor to the end of a windrow and lowered the hayfork attached to the front of the farmhand.

The hayfork was a monstrous pitchfork made of thirteen ten-foot-long wooden tines, six inches apart, with metal caps on the pointed tips. Above each outside tine were two more tines about eighteen inches apart. They formed the sides of the fork to keep the hay from falling off.

The tines moved along the ground like rigid tentacles and moved up and down only in response to small bumps or rocks. If a tine or tines met head-on with a mound of dirt or large rock, the least that would happen would be a broken tine. If speed was involved, major damage could be done to the hayfork and the farmhand.

Once the tractor and hayfork were lined up to the windrow, Dad pulled the gas lever and the tractor pushed ahead, louder and faster. The hay piled into the hayfork, pushing, bunching, and rolling layer over layer. Dad pursued a windrow until the hayfork was heaping. If you were close enough, you could see nervous grasshoppers escaping in all directions from the hay.

To maneuver the hayfork, Dad sent hydraulic signals from a lever located left and above his arm on the farmhand. To tip the front up, he pushed the lever back and down. That kept the hay from slipping out. With the front tipped up, he pulled out the lever and raised the whole hayfork a few feet off the ground. Then he drove to the haystack. The hayfork bounced with each little bump, giving the hay a bouncing ride to the stack.

Dad slowed the tractor and raised the hayfork to clear the stack frame as he approached. To raise the hayfork, the farmhand pushed black greasy cylindrical arms out of rigid hollow tubes attached to the lower back farmhand frame. Square arms were pushed from the square tubes attached to the top of the farmhand frame and connecting near the lower tubes to form triangles on both sides of the tractor. The rigid framework of the farmhand formed a square around the back of the tractor. The extending tubes raised the hayfork and pushed it ahead of the tractor so the hayfork would not end up above the tractor and dump its load of hay on the driver.

My job was trampling the hay. Carol and Kim were the "pitchfork men." They would spread the hay and shape the stack with pitchforks. The only tools I needed were my feet and my weight to press the hay down.

The three of us moved away from the section where Dad approached with the raised hayfork. None of us wanted an encounter with any of the tines heading our way.

When the hayfork was where Dad wanted it, he pushed the hydraulic lever forward and down. The hayfork tipped down and the hay fell on the ground inside the stack frame. Tipping the hayfork up to level position, Dad backed away, lowered the hayfork below his eye level, then revved the tractor and headed to another windrow to gather another load. His whistling carried through the air above the tractor's engine.

I watched Carol and Kim spread the hay, keeping out of the way of the sharp tines on their pitchforks.

There wasn't enough hay for me to trample yet. It would take several hayforkfuls to form the first layer on the ground.

I climbed to the top of the frame, which was as high as the top of my head, and sat down. I anchored myself with the heels of my

cowboy boots over one of the lower bars. The scratchy "swish swish" of the hay moved by the pitchforks was uneven. The rhythm of stacking wouldn't come until Carol and Kim warmed up. Away from the stack, the tractor engine revved, hummed, and stilled in turns as Dad erased another windrow with the hydraulic hayfork.

From my perspective on the frame, green fields stretched all the way around until the buildings of our farm blocked the horizon. Above the green fields, the sky was a pale blue dome over the whole prairie. Two popcorn kernel clouds floated slowly overhead. One gradually took the shape of a rabbit, then an elephant without a trunk lying on its side. As the cottony elephant started to rise, I heard the hum of the tractor behind me. I turned around and saw that the hayfork, in midair, was headed straight toward me.

Dad just can't stand to see me sitting, I thought. I scrambled down and moved to the opposite corner. The hay slid off the tines into a heap on the ground. A black cricket leaped out, then crawled under the horizontal stems, reluctant to give up its sweet aromatic nest of curing hay. Carol and Kim spread the hay around the stack floor. Carol's wide-brimmed hat shaded her face and an old long-sleeved blouse protected her arms. Kim and I wore nothing on our heads, and we had on old short-sleeved blouses that weren't nice enough to wear to school anymore. We wore the blouses outside our jeans. With all the arm movements, the blouses didn't stay tucked in anyway.

I thought about how it was too bad they didn't make overalls for girls — they're so practical for work and easy to put on. Dad left one strap hooked. The right strap, I bet. He slipped his arm through that strap and then pulled it up on his shoulder. He reached behind his back, brought the loose strap over his shoulder, slipped the wire loop over the metal button, and his shirt was automatically tucked in. Sometimes he left one or two of the three side buttons unbuttoned in hot weather. Like today.

Dad brought load after load of hay to the frame. Soon the whole stack floor was covered and the stack was on its way up. I was glad when my eyes were higher than the top of the frame. The view was better over the top than through the spaces between the bars.

When my stomach growled, I knew it must be close to noon and dinnertime. I was more than ready for a break and something to eat and drink. I saw Dad check the sun's position when he delivered a load. Finally, he called to Carol, "Take the pickup home and see

47

about dinner. Check the mail, too."

"Here, Rachel, you can have my fork," Carol said, smiling as she leaned the handle toward me. Her generosity didn't impress me, but the pitchfork was a welcome change from merely trampling the hay from one end of the stack to the other.

Carol drove the pickup across the field to the approach, then turned toward the county road to get the mail first. I watched her cloudy dust trail whip up faster after she turned on the county road and drove the mile north to the mailbox. Nothing else seemed to stir on the land.

"Don't you know how to use the pitchfork?" Kim chided.

"Well, why don't you just tell Dad I'm not working again," I retorted.

"I think he can see that for himself," she replied with a mocking grin on her face. She looked past my ear and backed away.

I turned to find the hayfork headed straight for me again. It was approaching in slow gear, so I had plenty of time to get out of the way, dragging the pitchfork behind me.

"The pitchfork works better if you use the tines instead of dragging it," Kim ridiculed.

"Oh, shut up!" I snapped.

Carol couldn't get back soon enough for me. Kim didn't pick on me so much when she was around. And I was hungry and thirsty.

8

It seemed like hours before Carol returned to the field with something to eat and drink packed in two small cardboard boxes. There was a thin band of shade on the north side of the haystack, and we ate there. We leaned our backs against the frame, and our legs and feet stuck outside the shade in the hot sun.

Carol handed Dad a couple of envelopes from the mail and kept the *Cresbard Beacon* to read. She had eaten at home so Mom would have less to pack. Dad laid the envelopes on the ground and took the half-gallon iced tea jar from the box.

"What's Mom doing?" he asked Carol before he lifted the jar to his mouth and swallowed the tea in big gulps.

"She was cleaning the oven when I got home," Carol said.

Kim got to the lemonade jar before I did. She took a long swig and said, "Boy, this lemonade hits the spot!" Instead of passing it to me, she drank more. And more.

"Save some for me!" I said. The anticipation of the tart lemonade made my mouth water.

She kept slurping and swallowing. I watched in fear as the level of the delicious drink fell in the jar. I was afraid that there wouldn't be any left. She must have sensed my breaking point because I was about to yell, "Dad!"

"Here!" she said, shoving the jar at me. I was horrified at the small amount that was left.

"Hog!" I mouthed at her. Then I made a big production of wiping

the jar rim with my shirt bottom to remove her germs before I drank. She wrinkled her nose at me, then turned her attention to the food.

The pale liquid with small pieces of lemon pulp and lemon rinds floating around was pretty to look at, maybe because yellow was my favorite color. It was still cold when I took my first swallow, and Mom had sweetened it just right. I took slow sips, savoring its goodness. I left a little in the jar, then put it on the other side of me behind my arm and in the shade. I would finish it after I ate.

Dad and Kim were eating their sandwiches. Dad had two double sandwiches. Kim had one. I reached into the box and retrieved one for myself. I folded back the waxed paper and the yeasty smell of fresh bread reached my nose. Summer sausage peeked between the two slices of bread. I lifted one edge of the sandwich, hoping there wasn't too much mayonnaise on it. There wasn't.

I was still eating my sandwich when Dad and Kim started eating their potato salad. Mom had packed Dad's in a pint-size Borden's cottage cheese container. Kim's and mine were in Blue Bonnet margarine tubs, about half the size of Dad's.

It didn't take Dad long to finish his potato salad. "Any dessert?" he asked Carol.

"Cinnamon cake," she answered. She reached into a box and produced three rectangles wrapped in waxed paper. One was twice as big as the other two.

"Your mother was busy baking this morning, girls," Dad said. "Fresh bread, fresh cake." He ate the soft cake with its sugar and cinnamon topping.

My mouth watered for the cake's sweet softness. Mom had spread butter on the top of the cake right out of the oven. As much butter as would melt into it. Then she sprinkled a mixture of sugar and cinnamon on top. But I had only begun my potato salad.

"Make sure you eat all your potato salad, girls," Dad said. "It won't keep in this heat, and I won't see it wasted."

I still had most of mine left, but cinnamon cake was on my mind.

"Do you want my potato salad?" I asked Kim, nearly mouthing the words so Dad wouldn't hear.

"Nope," she answered with a "hah-hah" grin on her face.

"Carol?" I asked, holding out the tub to her.

She shook her head.

Do I dare ask Dad? I wondered. Before I could ask, I had my answer.

"Eat that potato salad, Rachel," he said, looking at my container. "There's no cake until that's gone." Then he walked to the tractor.

The harshness of his words made me feel bad. I forced down the rest of my potato salad. The last bit of lemonade was all my stomach would hold. The lemonade seemed to have lost some of its flavor.

I climbed over the frame to the top of the stack. Carol and Kim were waiting for the next load. The sun was high and hot. I wished for my old cowboy hat so my face wouldn't burn. I wished for a breeze.

After the new loads of hay were spread over the stack, my legs sank into the hay about halfway to my knees. Each time I trampled over the hay, I sank less into it. Trampling was easier when I didn't sink so far.

The more the hay was packed, the more would fit into the stack. That's how Carol had explained it to me when I had asked once why the hay had to be trampled anyway. Dad was out of earshot, of course. She said that stacks on the field killed the alfalfa plants below them. Two stacks would kill more plants than one large one. She said something about fewer building materials and less time needed with larger stacks and compressed hay shedding more water, but I had heard enough explanation and quit listening.

All afternoon the loads of hay came. Sweat formed all along the hair by my face and around my neck. Carol and Kim had damp hair around their faces, too. The dry hot air evaporated the sweat before it could drip down our foreheads or temples.

Dad stopped for a drink of water and tossed the jar up to the stack so we could have a drink. The stack was now too high to reach the jar to us. The jar landed in the middle of the stack. Carol drank first, then Kim, then me. Dad waited below for the jar. I handed it back to Kim to toss down. I wasn't going to risk getting blamed if Dad missed it and the jar broke.

I thought about my cake and wanted it. *Would Dad toss it up to me if I asked him?* I wondered. I decided against asking. Besides, he was eyeing the haystack from a few feet away and had a displeased look on his face.

"Girls!" he hollered up.

We gave him our attention.

"This corner is starting to go in. Make sure you bring that out so the stack goes straight up."

"Okay!" Carol called down. Then Dad got on the tractor and headed for the windrows.

"It's just a haystack, for heaven's sake," Kim muttered. "Why does it have to be so perfect?"

Carol went to the corner and removed some of the hay, pitching it to the center. Then she started repitching that hay and building the corner straight. She was close to the edge, where the loosened hay was unpredictable. I had seen chunks of loose hay on edges break away and slide off the stack. Mom had almost gone down with some loose hay last year, but she had stabbed her pitchfork in some firm hay just in time to hold her.

I was leery of that corner. It would be hard to trample that hay and have it layer into the rest of the stack. Carol trampled it good herself.

She must have fixed it, because Dad didn't say anything about it when he brought the next load, and I saw him look at it carefully.

The afternoon dragged on. I was sure that this must be what prison was like—kept in a certain space all day long, forced to do something you didn't want to do.

When I looked out over the field, there were so many windrow rectangles, so many dark green hay rows on the light green and tan stubble field. Some of the rectangles had sides missing. Some two sides. A few of the large rectangles had been completely erased. But there were more windrows remaining than had been picked up. It would take forever to stack all that hay.

A lone cloud floated across the sky. I hoped it would pass over the sun. My hope faded as the sun inched westward and the cloud headed southeast.

I trampled hay, one heavy step after another. I wiped the sweat from my forehead with my arm and kept trampling. I was tired and hot and could go no further. I plopped down flat on my back, the way you do when making snow angels. The cloud had flattened, and wispy pieces were breaking away. The flat cloud drifted, placing itself between the sun and us. Its shade brought immediate relief from the sun and the heat.

I stood up and saw that the whole field had turned three shades darker.

"Doesn't that feel good?" Kim said.

"Does it ever!" Carol replied.

"Stay, cloud, stay," I commanded as though I could put a magic spell on it. But the cloud's real master—the wind—blew it away. The large shadow, a darkened island in the middle of sunny land, glided out of the field, over the farm, and off toward the southeast.

As the sunlight edged its way into the field and along the creek, Blackie emerged from the weeds by the creek bank and was highlighted.

"Blackie knows how to cool off," Carol said.

He was shaking the water from his coat after swimming across the creek. He must have gotten bored at home and decided to join the activity out here.

What a life! Free to go wherever he wants, I thought.

"Hiya Blackie!" I called, forming a megaphone with my hands.

He barked a reply. Then he sat in the shade near the pickup. Eventually, he lay down, rested his head on his front paws, and closed his eyes.

When Dad came with the next load, he told Carol it was time to go home and get lunch. It felt near four o'clock, the time we eat lunch on long workdays in the field. Supper would be after we got home.

The haystack was too high to climb down the frame, so Carol rode the hayfork down.

"Carol?" I called to her after Dad was on his way for another load. "Would you toss up my piece of cake? Please?"

"I'll try," she said. She threw hard to get the lightweight object that high. It was a good throw and I caught it.

"Thanks! Kim? You want half of my cake?"

"Sure," she said.

I was tempted to say, "Well, you can't have any," but a truce had settled on our bickering during the afternoon.

She devoured the soft cake in four bites. I kept my half cradled in the waxed paper to catch any crumbs. The cake was soft and delicious. Almost as good as it would have been at noon, when it was fresh and warm. I pinched the crumbs between my fingers and ate them. I crumpled the waxed paper into a wad and put it in my pant pocket.

When Carol returned, Kim and I jabbed the pitchforks into the hay so they would stand up. We rode down on the hayfork. The hard soles of my cowboy boots slipped on the smooth wooden tines. I gripped the frame, watching the ground come up to meet me. I held that grip until the hayfork rested on the ground and Dad shut off the tractor. Walking on solid ground felt funny.

Blackie came over, panting and wagging his tail.

"How ya doin', boy?" I scratched his neck and patted his head. "Good dog!"

There was enough shade on the side of the pickup, so we ate there. Dad sat on the seat with the door open. We girls found spots on the running board or ground.

Dad had devoured two of his four egg salad sandwiches by the time I took a waxed paper package. There were pieces of cake again, but no potato salad this time. The four o'clock lunch tides us over until suppertime, which could be after eight o'clock.

I ate my sandwiches, which were cut on the diagonal, forming two triangles. Blackie stood in front of me in anticipation. I planned to share a piece with him after Dad left, but then I realized that I would be up on the stack when that happened. Blackie might have to be satisfied with catching a gopher or field mouse for lunch.

There was no lemonade this time. There was cherry Kool-Aid, ice water, and iced tea, which was mainly for Dad. The Kool-Aid was sweet and good.

Dad finished his sandwiches and cake, then took a long drink of iced tea.

"You girls ready?" he asked. Then he saw that Kim and I were still eating. "Aw, never mind," he said, waving away the question. "I'll get a load and put it up there, then I'll hoist you up."

We were grateful for the extra rest.

"Do you think he'll pick up a far windrow or a close one?" Kim asked.

"I wish he'd get a far one, but I bet he'll get a close one," I said.

"Close," Carol said.

"Yeah. Close," Kim agreed.

We watched the tractor head away, the tines vibrating and the hayfork jiggling in delayed sync to the ground bumps.

Behind my back, I sneaked my last piece of sandwich to Blackie.

The tractor was still going. It passed a windrow.

"He's not getting the closest windrow," Kim said. "Not the second closest, either."

The farther the tractor went the happier we were. We were pleased, but surprised, that Dad drove to the farthest windrow in the field.

We sat completely in shade and rested, silent for a while. Blackie rested too, panting.

Kim broke the silence. "Is Mom still mad at Dad?" she asked Carol.

"I think so," Carol answered. "She wasn't very talkative. Susie made up for it though. She rattled on and on about wanting to come and help stack hay. Mom told her absolutely not."

"It's a good thing she isn't here," I said. "She'd only be in the way."

"She could help trample," Carol said.

"Yeah, but she doesn't weigh much," Kim said.

"And she gets tired too soon," I added.

"And she'd be one more thing to watch out for," Kim added. "As if we didn't have enough to watch out for already."

"What do you mean?" I asked.

"We have to watch so we don't fall off the edge of the stack. We have to make sure the edge goes up straight. We have to stay out of the way of the hayfork. We don't need a little sister to look after up here."

"I'm going to change the subject," Carol said. "Did you know there's a carnival in town tomorrow? I read about it in the *Beacon*."

"A carnival sure would be fun!" Kim said.

"Anything would be fun after this," I said.

A carnival came to town nearly every other summer, sometimes every summer. It was an exciting change from our boring routine.

The people were different. The rides were thrilling. Sometimes there were unusual animals. A tiger or two. An elephant or two.

"What do you think our chances of going are?" Kim asked.

"None, if Mom is still mad at Dad," Carol said.

We sat in silent disappointment for a while. Then Kim said, "Wait a minute! Let's not forget how helpful Susie can be in certain situations."

"Susie!" Carol and I exclaimed, wondering how we could have forgotten.

We talked quickly, for Dad was headed our way with a loaded hayfork. We thought of strategies to get Susie to say just the right thing to Mom or Dad. We decided to simply tell Susie about the carnival and let her work her little-kid charm.

We watched Dad raise the hayfork, drive up to the stack, lower the hayfork on the stack, then back away while the friction kept the hay there and the wooden tines came away clean.

It was time for our ride up. We spaced ourselves across the hayfork for balance, gripping the frame bar. The hayfork swayed a little as it went up. We stepped onto the stack and Dad backed away. Carol and Kim pitched the hay. I trampled.

The sun was on its way down. When I stood on the east edge of the stack, my shadow stretched tall and thin at the end of the long haystack shadow. I waved one arm, then both arms slowly, then both arms fast. I put both hands together and made long bird-head shapes with the shadow. The tractor with its farmhand and hayfork looked like a monster insect creeping toward the stack.

With each new load the shadows lengthened. The sunny areas faded. Across the creek at home, the large kitchen window over the sink reflected the bright red setting sun. The window lost its bright light and was colored red, orange, and pink from the western sky.

The shadows were gone. The bright light was gone. My eyes were grateful. The heat let up, but the hay was getting heavier as the evening dampness invaded the stems and leaves. The tractor worked harder to gather the loads. I heard it in the chugging motor. Dad brought a few more hayforks then announced, "Time to call it quits."

How good it felt to ride the hayfork down, although my stomach felt a tickle during the first few feet of the drop.

"That stack is getting up there," Dad said. I knew it was getting high, for Dad had looked smaller and smaller on his tractor as the afternoon had dragged on.

It was a relief to be done for the day. I didn't let it bother me that we had to come back tomorrow. My thoughts were on the carnival coming to town.

9

"Mama, don't you like Daddy anymore?" Susie asked in a sad little-girl voice. Her question came at the supper table after she had learned about the carnival coming to town.

Kim and I had told Susie about the carnival and described how fantastic carnivals were. She didn't remember the carnival from two years ago, and she was excited.

We had expected her to ask Dad about the carnival when he got to the table, but before we could stop her, she went directly to the bathroom where Dad was and bolted through the door.

Kim and I grimaced at each other, fearing that Susie would interrupt Dad at a crucial time.

"You girls look like you're up to no good." Mom's voice startled us as we waited just inside the kitchen door around the corner from the bathroom, out of sight but within hearing.

The guilt on our faces confirmed her suspicion, but Susie's voice interrupted before she demanded an explanation.

"Daddy, can we go to the carnival tomorrow night? Huh, Daddy?"

Susie was good! Her "Huh, Daddy?" oozed sweetness. How could he possibly say no?

After Susie's question, Mom knew exactly what Kim and I were up to. Mom's interest became as intense as ours. The three of us stood motionless, waiting for Dad's answer.

"How'd you know about the carnival?" Dad asked.

"Kim and Rachel told me."

"Oh, they did, did they?"

Kim and I rolled our eyes at each other. Now Dad would be on our case. But Susie persisted before Dad could yell for us.

"Yeah. They told me about the merry-go-round with fancy painted horses that go up and down and around and around. Please, Daddy?"

"Well," his voice was soft, like he was giving in. "Let's see if your mama wants to go. If she wants to go, then we'll go."

Mom's face soured when she heard that. She walked to the kitchen sink. Kim and I scooted to our places at the table before Dad and Susie came into the kitchen.

"Kid? You want to go the carnival in town tomorrow night?"

"Nope." Mom kept her back to him. She washed her hands to look busy.

"Mama, please. Let's go to the carnival," Susie pleaded.

"No. And I don't want to talk about it."

Susie stormed to the table and sat down with her lower lip pushed out in a big pout. She folded her arms across her chest. Her eyes filled with water, but she kept the tears from falling down her cheeks.

Dad called Carol from her room to come to supper before he sat down. All the food was on the table except the fried steak and the boiled potatoes in their jackets, which Mom brought and set in the middle of the table.

We folded our hands and bowed our heads in prayer. During the somber grace, I sneaked a peek at Susie. Her lips were quivering and she barely mouthed the words. A tear dropped on her green shirt, leaving a small dark spot.

I felt rotten.

We ate mostly in silence. Dad said something about the haystack getting pretty high and this was going to be a big one. "Mmmm," we said, nodding our heads just so there was a response.

Susie wasn't eating. Mom put a little of everything on her plate, but she just sat with her head down.

I avoided eye contact with Dad. I could tell he was upset with Kim and me for getting Susie's hopes up.

Eventually, Susie picked up her fork and started nibbling on some steak pieces that Mom had cut for her. After a few minutes, Susie asked that crucial question in her sweet, innocent voice: "Mama, don't you like Daddy anymore?"

Forks stopped, waiting for Mom's reply.

I guess Susie's unhappiness was too much for Mom.

"Oh, Sweetie," Mom said, pulling her toward her and comforting her.

Dad put a hurt puppy-dog look on his face and asked, "Yeah? Don't you like me anymore?"

A smile cracked the corner of Mom's mouth and then broadened. "Oh, you!" she said, waving off his antics.

"Can we go to the carnival now, Mom?" Susie asked, her face bright with hope and reverting to the grown-up version of addressing her mother.

"On the condition that I get a promise from you"—she looked Dad sternly in the eyes—"and your dad that you will not drive any machinery until you have *my* permission."

"Okay," Susie agreed quickly.

"Promise, Susie?"

"I promise. Cross my heart and hope to die." She drew the X on her chest.

"Kid?" Mom looked at Dad.

He hesitated.

"Daddy!" Susie cried in panic.

"Oh, sure," he gave in.

"Is that a promise?" Mom asked.

"Cross my heart," he nodded.

"You have to do the X, Daddy. The X," Susie reminded him.

Dad repeated "Cross my heart" and drew the X on his chest. "How's that?" he asked Mom.

"Good enough," she said.

"I can't wait to ride on the merry-go-round!" Susie said.

Kim nudged me slightly with her elbow as if to say, *We did it.*

"As for you two," Dad said, glaring at us. "If it weren't dark, I'd send you out to pull weeds along the fence line. Now clear the table and do these dishes for your mother. When you're done with that, you'd better hit the hay because we have a haystack to finish tomorrow before we even think about going to a carnival."

10

That night the wind came up. It was still blowing in the morning. Pieces of hay blew off the hayfork and rolled along the field, pushed by the wind. Dad brought smaller loads so less hay would blow away, and he drove more slowly to keep the wind from stealing chunks of hay.

The wind was from the northwest. Dad delivered the loads on the north side so the hay wouldn't blow back on the tractor and into his eyes. Instead, it blew toward the stack.

Carol, hatless today, and Kim had difficulty spreading the hay on the north side. The wind pushed back the hay on their pitchforks and blew it into their eyes. After they'd laid the hay in place and before I could trample it, the wind lifted chunks and threatened to blow them back on the stack. Carol and Kim stood on the chunks so the wind couldn't whip them away before I trampled them down.

Under calmer conditions, the haystack would rise by inches. Today, the stack rose by half-inches.

When Dad raised the hayfork, he did so slowly. When it was high in the air, the wind swayed the fork from side to side. Each time he approached, I watched in fear, wondering how much farther it could sway before something broke or tipped.

The wind stole tiny alfalfa leaves from the hay and swirled them in the air—so many that I was surprised to see some still on the stems when the hay reached the stack. The wind-driven leaves and hay flecks stung my face. I turned my back to the wind. The rush of

the wind in my ears lessened. If I held out my shirt as a parachute, I knew the wind would blow me off the stack.

Many windrows still lay in the field. I doubted that all the hay would fit into this stack. The stack was so high that the farmhand and tractor worked hard to hoist the hayfork to the top.

"Start topping it off, girls," Dad called after one tricky delivery.

It's about time, I thought.

Carol and Kim started pulling in the sides of the stack by pitching the hay in a few inches from the edge. They did this with each new layer.

The north side was easy to pull in. The wind helped. But it was hard to trample. The wind wanted to push it even more than Carol and Kim had planned.

"That looks like a big load Dad has this time," Carol said.

It was a big load for these high winds. The hay was piled higher on the hayfork than the other loads today, and the tractor crawled across the field with the fork in a low position. The real test would be raising it high enough.

"I hope he knows what he's doing," Kim said. "That last load was really swaying in the wind up here. The farmhand seemed to have reached its limit even when Dad revved the tractor motor."

Carol and Kim moved to the south side. I trampled with great care on that side, afraid of the wind with its strong gusts. When I looked down, the ground was far below.

Dad lined up for his approach to the stack. Slowly, the hayfork rose and extended. Slowly, the tractor inched forward. Kim and Carol were off to one side of where the hayfork would come and I was off to the other.

Higher and closer the hayfork came, swaying in the wind. Every muscle in Dad's body, which seemed small from up high, was tense with concentration, ready to make adjustments to avoid a mishap.

But he didn't have a lever to control the wind. A strong gust pushed the hayfork, and the force started tipping the tractor and farmhand. The right rear wheel left the ground. In a split second, Dad was off that seat and standing his weight on the right axle. But it wasn't enough.

I froze, my heart pounding, as the hayfork tipped toward me in slow motion.

"Rachel, get back!" Dad yelled.

I found my feet and stepped back, but the hay underfoot was loose and I tumbled backward on my rear. I saw the hayfork loom toward me as it tipped. I tried to push myself up but the hay wasn't firm enough. I turned over on my hands and knees and scrambled away, trying to stand up so I could run.

Suddenly, I was flat on my stomach, buried in hay and surrounded by darkness. And quiet. No wind. I couldn't hear the wind. Hay was in my mouth, my nose, my eyes. I closed my eyes and started digging out of the hay with my arms. When I gasped for air, hay was sucked into my mouth and nose. I did my best to hold my breath, flailing through the hay.

"Rachel?" I heard Carol yell.

"Here!" I yelled back. Hay filled my mouth when I gasped for breath after yelling.

Her pitchfork! She'll stab me with the pitchfork! I thought.

Something hard moved in the hay. It was biting at my arm. "Ahh!" I screamed.

"Rachel? Is that you?" I heard.

Then something grabbed my arm.

"Rachel, come this way." My arm was yanked until I was free of hay and free of darkness. There in the bright light was Carol gripping my arm.

I felt the wind on my back. I snorted hay from my nose, spit it from my mouth, and tried to blink it out of my eyes.

"Rachel, are you all right?" Carol asked, still holding on to my arm.

"I think so."

"Is she okay?" Dad called up.

"I think so," Carol answered.

Between blinks I saw that the hayfork had come to rest leaning on its side and anchored by the stack. The hay had tumbled out sideways on top of me. I kept spitting little pieces of hay, and my eyes were sore.

"If she's okay, I'm going home to get the M tractor to pull this over," Dad called from the ground.

"She's okay," Kim yelled. "Just has hay in her eyes and mouth."

"You girls stay on this side," Dad commanded, motioning to the windy side. "I don't think it'll tip any more, but if it does, it'll go with the wind." Then he added, "You hear?"

"Yes!" Carol yelled down.

We skirted around the hayfork to the windy side. Dad jumped in the pickup and took off. Even the wind didn't drown the noise of clanking tools and equipment in the box as the truck bumped across the field.

The wind rushed past my ears. My eyes ached. I coughed and spit hay and sneezed from hay dust.

"This could put an end to the carnival for us—if we have any more trouble," Kim said.

That thought had crossed my mind, too. I was looking forward to having a good time with my friends. I didn't see much of them during the summer, and we didn't have a telephone so I couldn't call them. Sometimes we wrote letters and sometimes I'd see them on Saturday nights. Still, it seemed that I had missed out on a lot when we returned to school in the fall.

"Let's sit down to get a little protection from this wind," Carol said.

She plopped on the haystack and sat cross-legged with her back to the wind. Kim and I followed suit. We built backrests with chunks of hay.

My sisters' faces were red from the wind and sun. My face was sore. When I pressed my hand to my cheek, it was burning hot.

I snapped an alfalfa stem and stuck it between my teeth to chew. Its earthy taste changed my mind. I decided it was a cigarette and pretended to smoke it, lifting my chin and releasing slow streams of smoke toward the sky.

Carol saw me. "Nice girls don't smoke," she said.

"Who said Rachel was nice?" Kim said laughingly.

"Don't you think you should be nice to me? I just escaped being buried alive in a haystack," I said. "How about a little sympathy?"

"You only had a little hay on top of you," Kim ridiculed.

"It felt like a lot of hay to me," I puffed, then held the alfalfa stem like a cigarette between my fingers. I was sorry it wasn't wheat straw, which is much better for play cigarettes. Wheat straw is hollow and you can suck in air before pretending to blow smoke rings.

I blew a long, slow stream of smoke, staring directly into Kim's eyes.

"Humph!" she snorted.

"Here comes Dad with the M," Carol said.

We watched him round the curve in the road. We knew he had the tractor in road gear, but it seemed to be crawling.

"I hope this pulls over easily," Kim said, "without anything getting broken."

It was the hope of all of us.

Dad brought two large chains with him. He parked the M sideways to the tipped tractor and farmhand and hooked both chains to the M's hitching bar. He clamped one chain around the farmhand's upper arm, close to the frame. He secured the second chain as high on that same arm as he could reach. Slowly he drove the M forward.

On the stack, we held our breath, waiting for the tractor and farmhand to respond. The first movement was a jerk. Then came a second jerk, which was followed by a slow backward movement as the hayfork began to level. The farmhand and tractor were slowly tipping back to flat ground position.

Slowly, slowly, the machine returned to an upright stance. The M growled as it pulled the resisting farmhand against the will of the wind.

Once on the ground, the big rear tire bounced and threatened to tip back, but the M held it fast. Dad secured the M's brakes and turned it off.

"How are you doing up there?" His question was carried by the wind.

"Okay," we called down.

"I'm going to lower the hayfork first," he said. "That will tilt the fork up and it should slide down the side of the stack a little."

Dad climbed onto the tractor and pulled out the lever. The hayfork did what Dad said it would.

The chains slackened as the arm lowered. Dad jumped off the farmhand tractor, started the M, and drove it just enough to tighten the chains again.

Some hay still remained in the fork.

"He'd better not ask us to pitch that hay off the fork," Kim said.

"I think it would be impossible," Carol said.

"What's impossible to us doesn't always seem impossible to him," Kim replied.

Dad looked at the hayfork, contemplating.

Surely he's not going to want them to pitch it on the stack, I thought. He seemed to be debating. I couldn't see, but I was sure he was rapidly blinking his eyelids under a furrowed brow.

Finally he said, "I'm going to bring this down with the hay in it."

"Well, I guess so," Kim said under her breath.

Dad backed the farmhand from the stack, lowering the hayfork as he went. The machine did not resist.

While he inspected the farmhand and hayfork, I asked, "How are we going to get down?"

"Good question," Carol said. "I don't see a ladder."

"All right, girls, top it off and trample it good," Dad called. "This stack is as high as it's going."

Carol and Kim pitched the last of the hay left from the tipped load to make a rounded cap over the top.

Dad drove the farmhand with the hay in the hayfork to a windrow. He bunched the windrow into piles to make it harder for the wind to scatter it across the field, as it was doing with many of the windrows—rolling sections of them out of line so they formed a dotted line.

The leftover hay would be hauled home in hayracks, large wagons framed in two-by-fours with spaces between the boards big enough for cattle to put their heads through. They were like small, mobile haystacks.

"If we have to haul the leftover hay today, we'll never make it to the carnival," I whined.

"First, we have to get down," Kim said. "We may be stuck up here forever. We may be up here until we die. We may not have to do another thing in our entire lives."

I didn't respond, just kept on trampling. Carol, too. We all trampled until the hay was packed. Then we trampled some more, hoping Dad would come back.

He finished bunching the windrows before he headed back. We waited, standing, looking down.

"Do you girls want down from there?" he called up, a grin on his face.

"How do we get down?" Kim asked.

"I'll hoist the hayfork with the tines up along the side of the stack. You should be able to slide down them to the frame bar." He tilted the fork up as straight as it would go, raised the farmhand as much as he thought safe, and drove the fork against the stack.

"Can you see the tines?" he asked.

We leaned over to look. The tips of the tines were several feet below the top.

"Work your way to the tines and then slide down them to the

attachment bar. Use your forks to steady you," he coached.

Kim and Carol edged backward down to the tines, using knee and toeholds and grasping their forks after jabbing them into the stack.

I watched them. It was a long way to the attachment bar. I pictured myself falling, rolling all the way down.

"We're at the tines," Carol said. "Come on, Rachel, slide down. We'll catch you."

"Oh, I don't know . . ."

"Come on. Dig your knees and toes into the hay and come down backward. I have a good toehold here, and I'm gripping the tines. Once you get down to the tines, it's easier," she tried to assure me.

"If you want to go to that carnival tonight, then you'd better start down," Dad said. He didn't mask his irritation.

I dug the left boot toe into the hay and bent into the stack with my knee. The right toehold was a couple inches lower. I repeated this very slowly, very carefully, hugging the stack with my knees until Carol could touch my foot.

"That's good. Now come down some more until you can grip these tines," Carol urged.

I lowered myself until I could reach down and grab the metal-capped point of two wooden tines.

"Good," Carol said. "Now, I'm going to move over here and use these tines and gradually work myself down."

She did. Kim was working her way down on the other side of me.

I straddled two tines between my feet and gripped each with my hands. I didn't notice that the hay scratched my fingers. I worked down the tines and hay a few inches at a time.

"Made it!" Kim cried with relief when she reached the frame bar.

"I'm down!" Carol announced.

"You're doing fine, Rachel," Carol encouraged. "Only three feet to go."

Suddenly, Dad started the tractor. I froze in panic.

"Well, don't take all day!" he ordered.

I was afraid he would back the tractor before I could get a good hold on the frame bar. I let myself fall to the bar and held on for dear life as the hayfork moved away from the stack and the tines leveled out straight.

In the spaces between the tines, the ground rose to meet me, rather quickly, I thought. It was a relief when the tines finally lay at rest on the flat ground.

But why had Dad been so impatient with me?

11

It seemed like the trip to Cresbard took a long time even though the speedometer read forty miles per hour. I looked back at the trail of dust billowing behind us on the county road. If a car was behind us, the driver would have to hold back in order to see and to avoid flying rocks from the gravel, which could crack the windshield.

When we turned onto the state road and passed a rise, the three grain elevators along the town's skyline came into full view. But what I wanted to see was the intersection of town, where the carnival would be set up.

We turned onto the half-mile road leading into town. It was hard to see from the back seat. I had to lean up and look over the seat and over an excited Susie, whose head was bobbing all over the place so she could see.

"There's the Ferris wheel, Susie!" I said, pointing at the tall wheel going around and around above the ground.

"Oooo," she said. "Where's the merry-go-round?"

"We can't see it from here," Mom said. "It's lower and goes around on the ground."

Susie watched the Ferris wheel. As we came closer she said, "There's people in those swinging seats up there, Mama." Her voice was high-pitched and excited.

The Ferris wheel stopped. "Why isn't it turning?" Susie asked.

"They have to stop to let people off when their rides are over," I said.

The Ferris wheel moved a bit, then stopped. "It keeps stopping," Susie said puzzled.

"The people in the bottom seat have to get out when the ride is over. They move the wheel to one seat and let the people out. They let the new riders in, then move it again to let the people out of the next seat. Over and over again," Mom explained.

"Now it's turning without stopping!" Susie watched in awe.

"Can I ride the Ferris wheel, Mama?" she asked.

"I think you'll like the merry-go-round," Mom said.

We passed the livestock sale barn and crossed the vacated railroad tracks. A couple of dust devils whirled and rose in the street, then chased each other into Way's Farm Implement yard. Dad parked our maroon 1953 Pontiac diagonally at the end of a long row of cars parked the same way.

Wooden sawhorses barricaded cars from entering the two main blocks of town. On the other side of the barricades, the carnival stood. Several light brown tents were on the street in front of Harris Meat Market, Osborne Barber Shop, and the Cresbard State Bank.

"I suppose you girls need some money," Dad said.

"Yup," Kim said.

Dad dug a wad of bills out of his front left shirt pocket and unfolded it. He handed a dollar bill to each of us in the back seat. I folded mine and put it deep in the pocket of my new red pedal pushers.

"What do you say, girls?" Mom reminded.

"Thank you," we complied.

"What about me?" Susie asked.

"I have your dollar, Susie. You'll stay with me," Mom said.

"But I want to go with Rachel," she said.

"No! You can't come with me!" I said emphatically. "I'm going to find Melissa and Winnie, and I don't want you tagging along."

"Well, aren't you the nice big sister," Dad said with disgust in his voice.

I didn't look at him, but I knew he gave me a disgusted look, too. I felt bad, but I didn't want Susie with me. Melissa and Winnie didn't have little sisters, so they wouldn't have any tagging along.

We got out of the car and walked through the space between the barricades. The ground was damp.

"Mama, they had rain!" Susie exclaimed.

"No, Susie. The town's fire truck sprayed the street to keep the dust from blowing," Mom said.

"Look, everybody! There's the merry-go-round!" Susie pulled Mom's hand to go faster.

The merry-go-round was the first ride beyond the tents. Susie led us past the sharp-shooting tent, past the fortune-telling tent, which had the door flap closed, past a weight-guessing booth, and past the Hercules booth.

"Look at all the horses! They're beautiful!" Susie exclaimed. She still held Mom's hand.

Mom and Dad smiled at each other as Susie stood in awe before the circling platform of carved horses with happy little riders. Brown horses, white horses, spotted horses, black horses and chestnut horses—fitted with fancy painted saddles and bridles—galloped around the platform, rising up and down on a pole that went from the ceiling to beneath the floor.

Carol and Kim went off to find their friends. I watched a complete round as the merry-go-round circled accompanied by organ music. I was hesitant to take off in search of Melissa and Winnie with Dad nearby.

"Mama, can I ride now?" Susie asked.

"You have to wait until it stops and you have to have a ticket," Mom explained.

Just then, Mr. Hall came by and Dad stepped back to talk with him.

Mom took Susie to the ticket stand and bought some tickets.

Now's my chance to leave, I thought.

"Rachel, buy your ticket!" Susie said.

"I'm not riding the merry-go-round!" I retorted.

"Rachel!" Mom used her disbelieving voice, then implored, "Ride with your little sister."

"Please, Rachel?" The anticipation and pleading in Susie's voice revealed how much she wanted me to ride with her. I was glad Dad didn't hear me say no to her.

"Okay," I agreed, managing to erase most of the disdain from my voice.

Mom gave me a ticket to ride. That brightened things for me. I wouldn't have to use any of my dollar for the merry-go-round.

"Choose the horse you want to ride, Susie, before it stops," Mom advised. Susie watched intently as the horses paraded around.

"That one!" Susie pointed to a white horse with a blue and gold saddle.

I hoped that no one would get it before she did when the merry-go-round stopped.

Susie clapped her hands when the white horse stopped near her. Mom helped her mount while I mounted a spotted horse with a gold saddle beside hers.

"Giddy-up!" Susie said. She learned that from playing Cowboys and Indians with me at home.

The music started and around we went. Up and down, around and around, up and down. Susie was thrilled. I liked it, too, but I hoped no one from my class would see me.

I watched from the corner of my eye for classmates because I didn't want to make eye contact and let them know that I knew they saw me riding this. I felt a little better when I saw some third-graders riding.

From the corner of my eye, I saw Dad at the Hercules booth. I turned my head to watch as he lifted the sledgehammer above his head and brought the hammer down with a mighty pound on the weight, which sent an iron cylinder up a pole to hit a loud bell. The people standing around clapped.

As the merry-go-round circled to the other side, Dad went out of view. When the merry-go-round returned, he was walking toward Mom with a stuffed animal under his arm.

"Daddy!" Susie yelled to get his attention. He smiled and waved, then went out of view. When we came around, Mom was holding a stuffed panda bear and Dad was heading across the street with a couple of farmers from our church. They were probably going to the pool hall for a game of pool or to play cards.

Good. Dad was gone. One ride with Susie was going to be all, and I didn't need Dad around to hear her beg me to ride again. I was anxious to find Melissa and Winnie and ride the Ferris wheel and the Tilt-a-Whirl. The Octopus looked fun, too.

"Rachel!" someone shouted.

It was Melissa and Winnie! Big smiles were on their faces, and they waved.

"Melissa! Winnie! Hi! This should stop soon," I called, turning my head to keep them in sight. As the merry-go-round circled, they went out of view.

"Wait for me so I can go with you," I called when they came back into view.

"Is the ride about over?" Winnie asked.

"Should be," I answered.

"Okay!" they said in unison. Both were wearing pedal pusher sets. Winnie's was red and Melissa's was blue. I felt glad that I, too, had a pair of the new-fashioned summertime pants that stopped mid-calf rather than below the ankle. My top didn't match the pants, though.

The merry-go-round slowed and the music faded.

"It's stopping!" Susie said with great disappointment. "Keep going! Giddy-up!" she ordered.

"The ride is over, Susie. We have to get off."

"No!" she persisted.

"Mama, I want to ride again. On this horse. Please?"

"Sure, Susie," Mom said. "Stay there and I'll get a ticket."

Melissa and Winnie were waiting for me, so I climbed down and told Susie, "'Bye!"

"Please ride with me again, Rachel."

"No, I'm going with Winnie and Melissa."

"Hi, Susie!" they said, waving.

"Aren't you going to ride the merry-go-round?" she asked them.

"No. We rode earlier."

That made me feel less foolish about riding the merry-go-round, which was a gentle ride and more for little kids.

Mom returned with Susie's ticket. She looked nice. She had on her new two-pieced navy maternity dress.

"I'm going with Melissa and Winnie, Mom."

"Okay. Now stay on Main Street," she said, "and be back by ten."

"I will." It was an easy order to obey. There wasn't anywhere off Main Street to go to.

"Rachel, why didn't you tell us your mom was going to have a baby?" Winnie asked.

"No big deal," I answered. "Have you ridden the Ferris wheel yet?"

"No. Let's ride that after the Octopus," Winnie said.

The Octopus had eight long arms with a closed-in seat at the end of each arm. The arms whirled around a center axle, moving up and down imaginary hills while the seats twirled.

We bought our tickets—twenty cents each. The three of us were small enough to fit in one seat. A man with a beard took our tickets and hooked our door shut.

At first it moved slowly, then it picked up speed. My stomach tickled on the down runs like it does when we're going fast down the hill on the county road. Then my stomach felt like it dropped away when the Octopus was at full speed. The rest of the carnival was circling around and around.

When the Octopus came to a stop, all three of us felt dizzy when we left our seat. We waited, laughing, for a few minutes before heading to the Ferris wheel.

"Rachel, have you seen David and Lance yet? They're here," Melissa said with a grin. Last year in fourth grade David was her boyfriend and Lance was mine.

"No, thank goodness," I said, indicating indifference.

"Don't you like Lance anymore?" Melissa asked.

"I don't know. He can be so obnoxious."

We stepped to the ticket booth and bought our tickets.

"Speak of the devil," I said behind my hand. "Look who's getting on the Ferris wheel."

There they were. David and Lance, climbing into a Ferris wheel seat.

"Hurry! There's no one in line. Maybe we'll get the seat after theirs," Winnie said.

We hurried and made it to the next seat. A dark-skinned man took our tickets and shut the side door after we were in. The seat moved back and up a little, then it stopped to load the next seat.

Something hit me on top of my head and tumbled into my lap. It was a crumpled paper gum wrapper wadded up with its tinfoil. "Hey!" I yelled.

When we looked up, Lance jerked back from the bar in front of his seat so we wouldn't see him. I figured he was the guilty one.

"Cut that out!" I called up.

"Yeah! Cut it out," Melissa joined in.

Lance and David's heads appeared over the bar. Wide grins were on their faces.

"What can we throw down on them when we get to the top?" I asked.

Winnie pulled some disc-shaped pink peppermint candies out of her pocket.

"Those will work," I said. "May hurt a little more than the gum wrapper. Aim for the tops of their heads."

We giggled in anticipation of our revenge. Three more stops—three more seats to fill—and we would be at the top, ready to drop candy peppermints on their heads.

At the top we leaned over and lined our sights with the tops of their barbered heads. I called, "Bombs away!" and we let them drop. Mine hit Lance, and Melissa's and Winnie's hit David.

"Bull's eye!" I shouted with satisfied glee.

"Just you wait! You'll get yours!" they yelled back.

"We're shaking," Winnie mocked.

The Ferris wheel didn't move forward at the expected time.

"Why aren't we moving?" Melissa asked.

It was then that I realized how high we were. The ground was far below. The people looked small down there. I could see the carnival with all its rides lit up and the stores along the street with their lights on, but I couldn't see directly below the Ferris wheel.

"Do you think it's broken?" I asked.

"What if our seat breaks and we fall to the ground?" Melissa wondered.

"Don't say that!" Winnie said. "There probably are slow people getting in and out."

"That slow?" I asked.

Our seat jerked but didn't move. It jerked again. We gripped the bar in front of us and looked at each other with wide, fearful eyes and pale faces.

A third jerk forced us against the front bar, and then we were moving down. No stops. Our seat passed the loading point and began the upward swing of its circle.

Somewhat collected, we decided the Ferris wheel was on a regular run. Still, a feeling of anxiety took some of the fun away.

A tickle ran down the middle of my stomach on the descent. "Ooooo!" I exclaimed, surprised at how much it tickled. The wheel picked up speed, the tickles grew worse. Each time we went down, I folded together, trying to shrink to bear the tickle in my stomach.

The Ferris wheel kept going around and around. "When is it going to stop?" I managed to gasp.

"It must be soon. We've been riding for a long time." Winnie was holding her stomach. Melissa leaned against her, gripping Winnie's arm.

Finally, the wheel slowed down. We were at the top when it stopped.

"It better not jerk this time," I said. We had forgotten about David and Lance. We risked leaning over the bar. They were still there.

"How'd you like that ride?" Winnie called.

"Piece of cake," Lance answered with a smug grin on his face.

"Yeah, I bet," Winnie said.

The Ferris wheel unloaded and loaded people without incident. We were relieved to be back on the ground. To our disappointment, we watched Lance and David walk away, following two giggling girls from last year's third grade.

"So much for Lance and David," Winnie said.

"Good riddance!" I said.

"Let's get a root beer float at John's," I suggested.

"Yeah, let's," Melissa agreed.

We crossed to the sidewalk, then passed the bank and the barbershop. We ran into Carol and two of her friends in front of Harris Meat Market. Carol had her eye to a hole in the back of a tent.

"What are you doing?" I asked.

"Shh." She turned to me and put her finger to her lips. "I'm watching the fortuneteller."

"Who's in there?" I asked in a whisper.

Carol moved away from the tent and whispered, "You can look now." She and her friends ambled up the sidewalk.

I rose on my toes to see through the hole—a gap in two seams of the tent. A girl in her teens dressed in flowing colored robes and a red scarf tied around her head held a man's hand with his palm outstretched. With her index finger, she drew lines in the man's palm.

"Let me see," Winnie said.

She watched for a while, then Melissa watched. We snickered at our cleverness.

I took another turn. The girl pulled the door flap back and the man left. She followed him out and a new customer entered. I was waiting for the fortuneteller to return.

"What do you think you're doing?" cried an angry voice. At the same time, my wrist was yanked and I stumbled back from the tent. It was the fortuneteller who gripped my wrist. Her eyes glared at me.

I was too shocked to reply. Winnie and Melissa cowered by the door of Harris Meat Market.

"Let go of my sister!" It was Carol. She and her friends had come back.

The girl still would not let go of me. She faced Carol defiantly.

"I said let go of my sister!" This time Carol, who was the same height as the fortuneteller, was face to face with her. Her friends were right behind her.

"I caught her peeping in my tent!" was the angry reply. She

yanked me again by my wrist.

"Ow!" I complained.

"Let go!" Then *smack*. Carol slapped her face.

This time, she let go of my wrist, hissed a word I couldn't understand but which didn't sound very nice, and returned to her tent.

"You okay?" Carol asked.

"Yeah," I said, rubbing a red wrist. Right then, Carol was the best big sister in the world. She examined my wrist, then she and her friends moved on.

Melissa, Winnie, and I moved on, too. We had had enough of tent-peeping. Besides, the seams had been rearranged inside and the peephole was gone.

The foamy mixture of root beer and ice cream tasted good. Our toes kicked the counter now and then while our feet dangled from the high stools in John's small, cement-block diner.

After fifteen cents for the float, I had forty-five cents left. Next I spent twenty cents for a ticket to ride the Tilt-a-Whirl. It was less thrilling than the Ferris wheel and the Octopus, but that was probably a good thing after the root beer float.

I parted with Winnie and Melissa and returned to the car a few minutes before ten. Mom and Dad were sitting in the car. Susie was asleep with her head leaning against Mom's shoulder.

Mom smiled at me. "She had quite a time on that merry-go-round."

Soon Carol came and then Kim moseyed along.

The three of us were quiet in the back seat. Tired, too. Carol and I would not tell Mom or Dad about the fortuneteller and her tent. There was a code among us siblings, and some things we just didn't tell our parents.

12

The carnival was a bright spot in my summer. So was Vacation Bible School for a week in late June. Five mornings in a row, Kim, Susie, and I went to the church in town. Five mornings in a row, I was free from farm work. Five mornings in a row, we squared off in an ongoing baseball battle during our morning break. The Bible stories were good, too.

During the next several weeks, we continued cutting, raking, and stacking hay in the fields around the farm.

The wild Angus were eventually turned out to pasture. They had gotten used to people coming and going when we fed them grain and hay.

We stacked tons and tons of hay, forming a huge, L-shaped stack in the yard where the Angus had been. Permanent frames served to hold the hay as well as fence the north and west sides of the yard.

Mom's stomach was getting bigger. Anyone who hadn't known she was pregnant could see it for sure now.

One day in late August, there was no need for me in the field and Dad told me to stay home with Susie and help Mom.

"You help her now!" he ordered. "Don't go running off to your room to read."

"I won't," I answered in an offended tone.

Why does he always assume I won't do my job? I wondered in a pout.

Mom asked me to dust the furniture in the living room. That was easy. Only a table, buffet, console radio, two lamp tables, and the tops of the baseboard heaters to dust. Then I dusted the floor in my room. Mom dampened the dust mop yarn first, and then I ran the mop over the bare floor and under the bed.

Susie was playing with her dolls by the bed and had to move her feet from spot to spot so I could get the mop under the bed. She kept her attention on her dolls and simply moved when I asked her or nudged her. I smiled when I had her move back and forth to the same spots several times.

"Mom!" She started her tattletale threat when she caught on.

"Okay! Okay! I'm done!" I left to dust the floors in the other bedrooms.

When the dusting was done, Mom sent me out with the wastebasket to burn papers and trash. I took two wooden matches from the red, white, and blue Diamond matchbox in the cupboard before I left.

I walked the thirty yards to the old oil drum we used for a burn barrel, dumped in the trash, struck the match against the rusty brown barrel, and held it to a piece from the *Aberdeen American News*. Instantly, the newspaper's edge turned brown and small flames ate a bite-size hole out of the edge before flaring. I stepped back when flames shot out of the top of the barrel, pushed toward me by the wind.

There was no need for the second match.

I watched the flames shoot up and bend, attempting to escape the inside of the barrel.

I should have placed the burn screen, which keeps the large burning sparks from escaping, on the barrel right after the fire started, but I was distracted by the leaping flames and just watched it for a while. When I reached for the screen, a gust of wind blew several burning pieces of paper up, out, and away from the barrel. They landed in different spots in the alfalfa field just a few yards away.

I put that burn screen on in a flash. Wisps of smoke rose immediately from the dry alfalfa, which lay like tinder waiting for a spark. The plants crackled as the wind fanned the smoke into flames. The spots were spreading fast. I tried to stamp them with my feet, but there were too many and the wind spread them too fast.

"Mom!" I yelled. I hoped Susie was still playing in our room and she would hear me through the open window facing this direction.

The fire was spreading, fanning in all directions and getting closer to the house.

"Mom!" I yelled again, feeling more desperate.

"She's coming!" Susie yelled from the open window.

Mom burst from the door with a wet towel in her hand. "Don't use your feet, Rachel! You might catch on fire!" she yelled to me. She slapped the wet towel on the flames that were spreading toward the house. She beat them out, but the fire was spreading into the field.

Blackie came around the house barking.

"I'm going to get your dad," she said. "This is too much for us. Get the bucket and fill it and keep beating the flames near the house with a wet towel." She handed the towel to me.

"Hurry, Mom!" I was afraid.

"Don't use your feet!" she ordered again.

As Mom was on her way to the car, Susie came out of the house. Mom grabbed her hand. "You come with me, Susie."

"I want to help Rachel with the fire," I heard Susie protest as Mom pulled her along.

I filled the bucket from the spigot jutting out of the basement, wet the towel, and struck at the flames in the grass around our house. The fire crackled and the black, burned spots grew larger as the orange and red flames ran ahead into the alfalfa.

I remembered the hose in the garage. I ran to get it and screwed the end on the spigot. I ran with the end toward the fire, which crept closer to the house. I squirted the flames. They hissed, died, and left smoke and black ground in their place.

I pulled the hose as far as it would reach and doused flames at the edge of the field. I was winning the battle near the house. Then the water from the hose slowed to a trickle and stopped.

I had emptied the house water tank! It would take hours for it to fill again. The water, which was piped uphill to our house from our slow-running artesian well, merely dripped into the water tank all day long. I didn't even have water to refill the bucket for wetting the towels, and the bucket was almost empty.

Stupid me for not putting that screen on right away! Our house was in danger of burning. And, Dad! Dad would want to know how the fire got started. Dread filled me as I fought the fire and feared the consequences of my stupidity.

Blackie kept barking. It was the only way he could help.

In minutes, Mom returned. "Dad is bringing the tractor home. He unhooked the mower and will try to plow a firebreak around the house and field."

She looked into the bucket. "The bucket's empty?" she questioned, then saw the hose. "You used the hose?"

I kept swatting the flames.

"The tank's empty!" she realized. "I'm going to Will's and have him call for the town's fire truck."

Susie was just coming out the door.

"In the car again, Susie!" Mom said.

"Where are we going this time?"

"To the Halls' to use the phone. Hurry!"

Mom zoomed down the lane and turned on the mile road just as

Dad came to the corner with the tractor, gas wide open in road gear. The big back wheels were turning so fast their large treads created a blur. Dad drove past me to the tree windbreak behind the tractor garage where the plow was parked.

The flames were moving along the edge where the alfalfa met the grass of our yard. I swatted them with the towel, dampened by the last bit of water in the bucket. The fire was burning its way deep into the field, already halfway to the east road where power poles and a power line had just been installed last year.

I felt the heat of the flames on my face. The heat dried the towel. The edge of the towel scorched. The dry towel was useless. It would only catch fire and spread the flames.

Dad was back with the plow hitched behind the tractor. He lowered the plow and revved the tractor. Clumps of dry brown sod turned over and traded places with the alfalfa plants. Dad plowed around the edge of the field where the alfalfa and our grassy yard met. He plowed back and forth a couple of times to make a wider firebreak.

The flames probably would not jump that firebreak, but the wind was chasing the fire across the field and it was getting closer to the east road and the power line. Dad plowed through the field near the edge of the fire, heading out and around so he could get ahead of it before it reached the road. It seemed that the tractor crawled while the fire raced.

I watched, holding my breath, while Dad plowed along the road, reaching the farthest point of flames just in time. The flames stopped at the turned-up sod and died, leaving a field of black behind. Dad plowed around the perimeter of the flames to where he had begun. The firebreak had stopped the fire from spreading. While the fire burned inside the firebreak, Dad watched from his seat high on the tractor.

Mom returned and stood by Dad's tractor, watching. I stood close to the house. Blackie, beside me, had stopped barking.

"Here comes the fire truck!" Susie exclaimed.

The red truck rounded the bend as fast as it could with that swishing water that it was carrying. Blackie ran barking to meet the truck when it turned into our lane. He chased the back tire until the truck stopped near Dad.

Mr. Arndt and Mr. Green from town jumped out. Dad got off the tractor and met them. "It looks like we have it under control, boys," he said.

"The wind was pushing it pretty fast and I wasn't sure we could stop it," Mom added.

"Well, I'm glad it's contained," Mr. Arndt said. "We'll extinguish the flames at this end of the field close to your house and as far in as we can until our truck is empty."

They rolled out the hose and turned the truck pump on. Mr. Arndt aimed the nozzle at the flames, which were burning low to the ground now. I watched the streams of water reduce the flames to hissing patches, which turned into wisps of smoke curving along the ground.

"How did it start?" Mr. Green asked Mom.

"Some burning papers got away from the burn barrel," she answered.

"Got a screen for the top?" he asked.

"We do." Then she assured him, "We'll check out why that wasn't on and exactly what happened."

"That's the end of our water," Mr. Arndt called in the middle of the blackened field.

Mr. Green helped him roll the hose on the truck. When they left the yard, Blackie barked his farewell while chasing the tires.

Dad started walking toward the house. "How did this start?" he asked. He looked at me for an answer.

I swallowed but couldn't give an answer.

"Wasn't the screen on the barrel?"

I was afraid to answer with the truth, and I was afraid of what might happen to me if I lied.

Susie helped me out.

"Rachel was watching the fire and some burning papers flew out. Then she put the screen on." Susie's words were more a report than a tattle.

"You didn't put that screen on right away? And it was windy?" he demanded, his anger rising.

I stood with my head down. I didn't nod. He knew the truth anyway.

"You . . . you almost burned our house down!" he shouted. "And look at the alfalfa that's gone!" He was getting angrier and could hardly speak.

"Kid, come in the house for a while," Mom urged. "Have some iced tea. It's hot and you can cool off a little. We've had a close call."

"This isn't the last of this, Rachel," Dad said, shaking his head while following Mom. "You have to learn something, someday."

"Kid," Mom pleaded.

Mom, Dad, and Susie went into the house. I stayed behind, my head still down. If I were to lift it, the tears would drip down my dusty red cheeks. I sat on the grass, quivering at the memory of the near tragedy, wishing it was a nightmare and I would wake up. I wondered what my punishment would be. *This isn't the last of this*, Dad had said.

After a few minutes, Susie came out with a glass of lemonade for me. She had one for herself, too. She carried them carefully, watching the tops so they wouldn't spill, as she walked over the lumpy grass.

"Mom sent this for you," she said.

"What are they talking about in there?" I asked, taking the foggy glass.

"I don't think you're going to get to go to town Saturday night," Susie said.

"I don't care," I shrugged. But I really did. Saturday night in town was blessed relief from this place in the summer.

13

Susie was right. Dad decided that I wouldn't go to town Saturday night and while everyone else was gone I had to pull weeds.

"You'll pull the weeds around all three steel buildings, the tractor garage, the chicken house, the granary, and if you get those done, the corn crib," Dad said when he dished out my punishment.

The weeds were hard to pull. The ground was so dry the roots wouldn't come out. Instead, the stems broke off at the ground, leaving the roots to grow again and to be pulled again.

If I weren't being punished, this would have been done another time and I'd have had help and someone to talk to.

Dad told me to start with the steel buildings. Then he, Carol, Kim, and Susie got in the car and headed for town.

Mom claimed she wasn't going because she didn't feel energetic enough. I think she felt a little sorry for me and stayed home so I wouldn't be there by myself.

The round steel buildings were painted silver last year, so I was glad it was evening. The sun was not directly overhead to create a glare and reflect light to burn my face.

My palms were red and sore from tearing off the tough dry weeds. There were no tender, juicy green stems like those that grew when there was plenty of rain.

After a while, I got tired of kneeling and decided to sit sideways on my bottom to rest my knees. My grip was not as strong in that position, so I knew I couldn't stay that way very long. I wouldn't

make enough progress to escape Dad's displeasure.

The change of position felt good, though, and I relaxed, feeling less resentful. My shadow was wavy on the corrugated metal of the steel buildings. The sun, low in the sky, was still warm on my back and neck. Blackie ran between the buildings, his nose to the ground, on the trail of some small animal. I heard a pheasant call in the distance, too far away to hear the beating wings of its short flight.

A gopher, scampering between the steel buildings, stopped, stood on its hind legs, front paws dangling, looked at me, listened, and then ran away.

Boom! The loud explosion in the sky startled me. It was one of those sonic booms from a fast-flying jet. We had been hearing sonic booms regularly when planes from the Rapid City Air Base held training flights.

"Ouch!" A sharp sting at the top of my leg made me yell. Then another sting near the first one made me get up. More sharp stings spread across my leg. The stings itched and I scratched them. Then I saw the tiny red ants crisscrossing all over my pants, and I knew I must have sat on an anthill. Sure enough, under the matted brown grass where my behind had been, was the flattened mound of tan soil with ants running around in all directions.

The stings were unbearable. "Ouch! Ouch!" I had to get rid of those ants. I removed my pants as fast as I could and brushed the ants off my legs.

The stings spread to my fanny. My underpants would have to be taken off. I didn't like the idea of taking them off, but I did. I shook the underpants to knock off the ants. I turned them inside out and shook them again.

I slapped a few more scurrying ants off my legs and a couple more that were exploring my stomach. Embarrassed by my nakedness, I hurriedly put on my underpants.

I held up my pants and saw lots of ants running around in confusion. I shook the pants hard. When it looked like the ants were off, I turned the pants inside out and shook them again. I examined them carefully before putting them on.

I stepped back from the anthill and leaned over, watching them frantically moving in all directions. From their point of view, I had invaded them by sitting on their mound.

I gave them space and moved farther around the steel building. I moved the matted grass apart to make sure there weren't more anthills, kneeled toward the shiny corrugated wall, sighed, and continued my punishment.

Before long, I thought I heard a faint voice calling, "Rachel?" I stopped and listened. It must have been my imagination. I pulled more weeds, breaking their stems near the ground.

"Raaachel?" It was a faint echo off the side of the next steel building. I stopped pulling. The echo came again. It sounded like Mom's voice.

I ran to the side of the chicken house so I could see the house. Mom was on the cement drive, hugging her huge stomach. Something was wrong.

"I'm coming, Mom!" I ran as fast as I could.

"What's wrong?" I asked, gasping for breath.

"I . . . think it's time . . . for the baby."

"The baby? It's not supposed to come yet."

"You have to drive me to the hospital . . . now, Rachel. This baby is not . . . going to wait."

"But I've never driven the pickup, Mom."

"You can do it. Now help me . . . get in."

I lifted the garage door. The pickup was so close to the door, I wondered how would I be able to back out without hitting it. The passenger side had plenty of room because the car was usually on that side.

I opened the pickup door for Mom. She moaned as she lifted herself up the high step and into the pickup. She moaned when I shut the door.

I looked with dread at the few inches between the pickup and the side of the garage door when I hurried to the driver's side. The door was heavy, and it was a high step for me to get in.

Mom moaned again.

97

"Mom, are you okay?"

"I've got a baby here that's anxious to be born, Rachel. Ow! We can't waste any time."

I knew Mom had to be in a lot of pain because she was not a crybaby.

It was a long stretch for my foot to the gas pedal. The steering wheel was higher than my eyes. The key was in the ignition because Dad always left it there.

"Make sure it's not . . . in gear," Mom said and then moaned.

I checked. "It is in gear!"

"Push in the clutch and move the gear so it's . . . in the middle and moves around."

I did that.

"That's right. Ooooh! Ow!" Mom doubled over.

The pickup started to slowly back out the door.

"Mom, it's rolling!"

"That's okay. Don't turn . . . the steering wheel and it should roll . . . oooh . . . straight back."

As it rolled back, I saw the side of the garage door very close outside my window. I gasped when I realized the rearview mirror was sticking out too far. It scraped the side of the door and bent back, leaving a big nick in the white-painted wood.

When we were to the end of the drive, I turned the wheels, backing into the road and heading away.

"It drives like the tractor . . . except for the gas pedal," Mom coached.

I turned the key and the engine started. I stretched my left foot and pressed in the clutch so I could put it into first gear. The pickup jerked and then died when my foot slipped off the clutch.

"Oh, Mama," I cried in apology.

"That's . . . okay. Try again."

I sat on the very edge of the seat to reach the clutch better. I pushed in the clutch again and started the engine. I let out the clutch slowly and the pickup headed down the lane.

"Do you think . . . you can shift to second? We . . . have to go faster."

I pushed in the clutch like the tractor and shifted to second gear. "*Graarr!*" The grinding gear vibrated through me. I moved the gear a little more to the right and forward and it went in. I held my breath as I let out the clutch. I released a sigh when the pickup moved on smoothly, faster now. I maneuvered the right corner and rounded the curve, continuing in second gear to the county road.

When we neared the county road, I asked Mom, "Can I go to Halls'? Maybe one of them could drive us?"

"No, Rachel. If they're not home . . . we'll lose . . . precious time. I don't . . . have much time."

Since nothing was coming on the county road, I took the corner rather fast. I didn't want to risk shifting down. Mom was flung against the door.

"Oooh!" I scolded myself and apologized in the same word.

"You're . . . doing . . . fine . . . Rachel." Mom resettled herself on the seat with difficulty.

There was a two-mile stretch south until I had to make a right turn. It was a good time to shift to high gear and go faster.

I felt sorry for Mom. I wished I could take her pain away.

In preparation to shift to high I prayed, "Please, Dear God, let this gearshift *shiiift!*"

It did. No grinding. Then I pressed the gas pedal down. The speedometer needle pointed to 40. Then 50. That was as far as I could push the pedal.

Please, God, help me get Mama to the hospital in time, I said to myself.

The steering wheel vibrated in my hands. I held it as steady as I could. I drove in the middle of the road to avoid the loose gravel along the side. I hoped we would meet someone and I would flag them down for help.

"Mom?" I called, keeping my eyes on the road in the open space below the top of the steering wheel.

"I'm okay. Keep going . . . just like you are."

I rounded a curve. Hard ripples in the road made the back end of the pickup swerve, but I kept it on the road. The right turn was ahead. I slowed down. No cars were coming from either way, so I

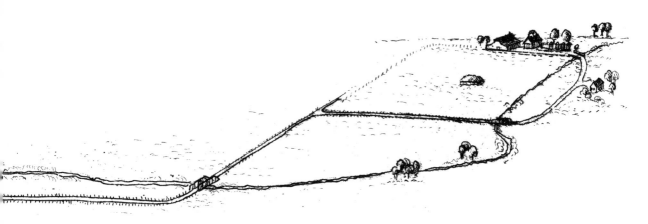

slowed to twenty-five miles per hour and didn't stop. Mom was flung, moaning, over by me. The pickup jerked and sputtered. It kept jerking little jerks like it was coughing. Then it recovered and moved on.

Mom pushed herself upright on the seat again.

I pressed the gas pedal as far as I could. The needle went to 50. The three miles driving west were fine. The intersection with the state highway was my next fear. I hoped I wouldn't have to stop again, even though there was a stop sign. Shifting this pickup was tricky for me. If I had to stop, I'd have to start from first gear again.

"Ow! Ow! Oh, Rachel . . . hurry!"

I pushed my toe as far as it would go. The needle reached 55.

"Okay, Mom." I tried to use a calm voice to comfort her.

A car was coming from the north and south on the highway. At their speed, it looked like they would be past when I got there.

I took the corner without stopping. It didn't work. The pickup jerked along for a way then died.

"Oh, no!" I said aloud. *Please, Dear God*, I said to myself.

"Mm . . . mmm," Mom moaned.

I turned the key and the pickup started. The gearshift complained again in a loud grinding noise until I found the right spot. I let out the clutch slowly and the pickup moved ahead. The shifts to second and high were easier.

We were a half-mile to the Faulkton turnoff. I was glad that the year before they had made a curve joining the Faulkton road. No stop sign.

"Two more miles, Mom," I said, hoping it would comfort her.

"Good, Rachel . . . good."

I stretched my foot and toe. The needle swung to 40, then 50, then 55. The paved highway was much smoother than the gravel roads.

The grain elevators at the edge of Faulkton grew larger.

"We're almost there, Mom."

"That's . . . good. Oh! Ow!"

I slowed to forty when the pickup reached the elevators. "Two more blocks to the hospital street, Mom," I reassured her.

At the hospital street, I turned left. The pickup jerked but didn't stop. Two more blocks. I decided to clutch and shift the gear to neutral. That way it would coast the last block and I'd use the brake to stop it. I thought it would be too hard to press the clutch and the brake at the same time.

I guided the coasting pickup near the hospital sidewalk. I turned the ignition off. "Mom, I'm going to run in and get someone. Be right back."

"Yes . . . hurry."

I raced across the lawn to the hospital door. A lady in a white dress was seated at a desk near the door.

"Come quick! My mom's having a baby in the pickup!" I yelled.

14

"Is my mom all right?" I asked the lady in white behind the desk that said REGISTRATION. Her nametag said NURSE JANICE HANSEN. She was dressed in a white cap, a white dress, white nylon stockings, and white shoes.

"She'll be fine," she answered, smiling at me. "She's in the delivery room now having her baby.

"You're such a brave little girl to be able to drive that pickup here the way you did," she added.

"Hmm," I replied, not paying much attention to her praise because I was worried about Mom.

"I telephoned the Cresbard pool hall," she continued. "Your dad was there and they gave him the message. He'll be here soon."

I went back and sat on the squeaky, wiggly wooden folding chair. I figured it would be about fifteen or twenty minutes before Dad and my sisters arrived.

The people at the hospital had been very fast when they wheeled the gurney out to the pickup, strapped Mom onto it, and ran her back into the hospital.

On this chair, my feet didn't rest on the floor. Only my toes touched the floor. Any movement I made caused the chair to wiggle and squeak. I crossed my legs and the chair wiggled and squeaked. That wasn't comfortable, so I uncrossed my legs. The chair wiggled and squeaked again.

The man reading *Look* magazine across from me lowered it and looked at me over the top of his reading glasses. I looked out the window and held my breath so I wouldn't move.

It was almost dark outside. I was glad that there was still some light when I'd had to drive the pickup into town.

"Ouch!" I grabbed the side of my leg, practically falling off my chair. That was a familiar pain. A red ant had to be in my pants yet.

The man gave me a disgusted look.

"Ant!" I explained. "There's an ant in my pants." I ran to the restroom. I quickly took off the pants and examined them. I saw an ant scurrying along the cloth. I squashed it with vengeance under my thumb and flicked it away. I looked over the pants hurriedly because I wanted to be out there when news of Mom came.

I returned to my squeaky chair. The man had resumed reading the *Look* magazine.

"Aaaa!"

Our three heads went up and we held them still, listening.

"Aaaaa!" It came again.

"Sounds like you have a new baby in your family," Nurse Janice Hansen said.

"How is my mom?" I asked.

"I'm sure she's all right. They'll be out to talk to you soon."

The clock had moved from 8:25 to 8:35 since I'd been sitting in that room. It took forever for it to move to 8:40. Then 8:45.

Another nurse, dressed in white from top to bottom, opened the door to the waiting room. "Rachel, your mom wants to see you," she said, holding the door for me.

My heart was beating fast. I didn't know how Mom would be. She wasn't very good when she was wheeled into the hospital.

I followed the nurse to a room with an open door. She walked in and I followed her.

"Here's your daughter, Mrs. Johnson," the nurse said.

"Mom!" I exclaimed as I dashed around the nurse and to her bed.

"Hello, Rachel," she said weakly, but smiling. She was sitting up in bed. She held a baby, bundled in a blue flannel blanket. "You have a baby brother."

"A baby brother?"

"A baby brother," she affirmed.

"He's so red and wrinkled," I said, looking at his tiny face with closed eyes and curled fingers beside his cheeks.

"All babies are at first," Mom said.

"I'll take him to the nursery now, Mrs. Johnson." The nurse leaned over and gingerly took the blue bundle into her arms. "You get some rest."

"Soon," Mom replied softly.

"Mom, are you all right?" I asked after the nurse left.

"Just tired," she sighed.

"Rachel, my brave girl." She smiled and ran her cool hand across my forehead and down the side of my hair. "We made it just in time. Your baby brother is alive because you got us here."

"Hmm." I smiled back at her. She looked very tired.

"Mama, you sleep now like the nurse said. I'll sit here in this chair by you until she makes me leave."

"Yes, Doctor," she teased. Then she closed her eyes. Soon I heard her sleep breathing.

I sat back on the chair, glad it wasn't a squeaky, wiggly one, and wondered how long it would be until everyone else was here.

The next thing I heard was, "Wake up, Rachel. We're here!" Susie was shaking my shoulder when I opened my eyes.

"Hi!" I said. Everyone was in the room—Dad, Carol, Kim—and Mom was awake.

"Let's go see our baby brother," Susie said, pulling my hand to get me off the chair. "Come on, Carol, Kim!"

"We already saw him once," Kim protested, but she came along.

We walked down the hall to the nursery. Only one baby was in the nursery, and he was sleeping in a bassinet in front of the big window. A tag on the bassinet read BABY BOY JOHNSON.

"There he is! There's our baby!" Susie said. We looked at the doll-size human held snugly beneath the blue flannel blanket, tucked securely under the corners of the bassinet mattress.

"At least it's a boy this time," Kim said.

I left to go back to see how Mom was doing. Susie had pulled me away before I could really see her.

I heard Mom talking in a low voice as I approached the door to her room. It seemed like a private conversation between Dad and her, so I hesitated before going in.

"The baby was born eight minutes after we got here, Kid. The umbilical cord was wrapped around his neck." She was speaking in a low voice, but emphatically. "He never would have lived if we hadn't made it here for his birth." She paused, then said, "Rachel was such a brave girl!"

"To think that I almost changed my mind about making her stay home because I, and you, thought I was being a little hard on her," Dad said. "Then she would have been in town with us," he said, pointing out the obvious.

"She had a little trouble driving that pickup," Mom chuckled weakly. "I know it's not funny, but the pickup jerked a lot and then it stopped on her a couple of times. She must have been hysterical inside, but she kept her composure."

"We were lucky this time, Kid," Dad said.

I knew that conversation wasn't meant for my ears, but I couldn't walk away because I was afraid they would hear my footsteps. I tried to comprehend what Mom said about the baby and how brave I was. Driving the pickup while she was in agony seemed like a bad dream to me. It was hard to remember the details.

I was surprised to hear Dad say that he was a little hard on me. I felt he was hard or harsh with me often, and now it sounded like he didn't mean to be and he was sorry.

"Rachel, come here! Come look at him! He's waking up!" Susie exclaimed.

When I turned to walk down the hall to keep Susie quiet, I heard Mom say, "What shall we name our baby boy?"

"He's opening his eyes!" Susie said.

"It looks like it's hard for him to open his eyes," Carol said. His lids slowly lifted, then he closed them again.

"Maybe the light hurts his eyes," I said. "After all, he has been inside Mom's stomach, where it's dark, for a long time."

"Rachel?" It was Dad calling from the door to Mom's room. He motioned for me to come. "Your mother wants to see you."

"Yeah?" I asked when I approached her bed.

"Dad and I like the name Matthew for the baby and we thought we'd let you pick his middle name."

"Oh! Gee!" I stammered.

I thought for a minute while they looked at me and waited.

"Lee. I like Lee."

"Matthew Lee it is then," Dad said.

"Matthew Lee is a wonderful name. Thank you, Rachel," Mom said.

15

In a couple days, Mom came home with Matthew Lee. He was wrapped in a blue and pink plaid flannel blanket, a leftover from Susie, or even me.

Mom said he was a good baby. He didn't cry a lot and he woke up only once in the middle of the night to be fed until he was six weeks old. Then he slept through the night.

Carol, Kim, and I did have to help take care of him once in a while. Mostly we changed his diaper now and then, but only wet diapers. Mom usually changed his dirty diapers because we girls wrinkled our noses and made such a fuss about the smell. Mom decided it was just easier to change those herself. But she reminded us that once we were all babies who had dirtied our share of diapers.

Sometimes I felt a little ashamed of myself when I grumbled about helping, especially when I remembered that I had gotten to choose his middle name.

We entertained him if he got fussy when Mom was busy making meals. Susie was good at that. Matthew enjoyed her animated movements, and she sang songs to him, like "Jesus Loves Me" from Sunday school.

Summer vacation was coming to an end, and I was glad. I missed my school friends in the summer, and, of course, the schoolwork was more fun than the farm work.

By the end of August, all the hayfields had been cut and stacked. The workload was easier. Had there been more rain, we would have done it twice. The next big work time would be in October—corn-picking time. Until then, we sorted cattle, separating calves from the cows and separating fat feeders to sell. Even the wild Montana cows acted like they were at home among us.

I tried to be brave when we worked with the cattle, but it was hard. They were such big animals. They still frightened me.

I didn't do so many stupid things anymore, like burn the alfalfa field near our house.

One day, Dad trucked a load of cattle to the Cresbard Sale Barn. I heard him tell Mom, "I need to deposit more money into our bank account. The girls will need some new clothes for school."

I asked if I could ride along and go to the library. He said I could.

Dad never said anything to me about the day I drove Mom to the hospital. Nothing like, "What a fine thing you did," or "What a brave girl you were," like Mom did. Still, I think he was appreciative because he seemed to have a softer way toward me. He cut me a little slack if I didn't do something just right the first time.

We didn't talk much on the way to town. He usually didn't unless Mom was along. He noticed I had comic books.

"Comic books?" He sounded disapproving.

"Comic books, and *Little Women* and Nancy Drew," I replied, pointing out the books.

At the sale barn, he backed the truck to the unloading chute. I got out with my books and comic books to return to the library.

Dad looked over the stockyards. "Doesn't look like too many cattle here today. If the sale doesn't last long, I'll be at the pool hall. Check there before you walk all the way out here."

"Okay."

I browsed at the library in the basement of the Masonic Lodge building for about an hour. I chose some comic books, despite Dad's disapproval. "Archie and Veronica," "Wonder Woman," "Superman"

111

for me. "Little Lulu," "Donald Duck," and "Porky Pig" for Susie. I checked out another Nancy Drew book, *The Secret of Red Gate Farm.*

Dad's truck was parked along the street opposite the pool hall, so I went in to let him know I was back from the library. The smell of smoke, beer, and dust mingled in the air. Dad was in the middle of a card game with three other men.

"Would you like some pop?" he asked.

"Sure." He got a dime out of his pocket and gave it to me.

"What'll it be?" Mr. Albee asked as he lifted the lid to his pop machine.

"Pepsi Cola," I said.

Mr. Albee took hold of a Pepsi Cola bottle top and slid it to the end of its row where it could be lifted out. Then he lowered the lid and removed the bottle cap from the tall glass bottle using the fixed opener at the front of the machine.

I gave Mr. Albee the dime Dad had given me and went outside. The door was propped open. I sat on the sidewalk and started reading the Wonder Woman comic book. The Pepsi Cola stung my throat. It felt good and the sweetness tasted good. I took a big swig from the bottle.

"Ha! Trumped you on that one, Chester!" I heard Dad say.

"How's that new baby doing, Tony?" one of the men asked while the cards were being shuffled and dealt for the next hand.

"He's doing real good," Dad answered.

"Must be great having a boy after all those girls."

I was half-listening until that comment. I put the comic book on my knees, set the pop bottle on the sidewalk, and waited for the answer.

"I don't have *any* complaints about my girls," Dad said.

"I've seen Tony's girls in action. They can work as hard and drive those farm machines as well as any boys," one man said.

"I heard that Rachel out there drove your wife to the hospital," Mr. Albee said.

"She sure did," Dad said. "And she had never driven that pickup before."

"That's really something," Mr. Albee said.

"It certainly was," Dad said.

"Yup! I'm real proud of my girls!"

Epilogue

The last few days of that summer, I tried hard not to goof up in any way. I can't say that I liked the farm work any more than before, but I kept my grumbling to myself. I was nice to Susie and I helped cheerfully with Matthew Lee.

It's a good thing that summer was almost over. It's hard to be that good for very long.

Dad was still a little short-tempered from time to time, but it didn't bother me the way it used to. I had heard him say how he felt about his daughters.

And when school started, I'm sure I was the happiest fifth-grader in Cresbard, maybe even in all of South Dakota.

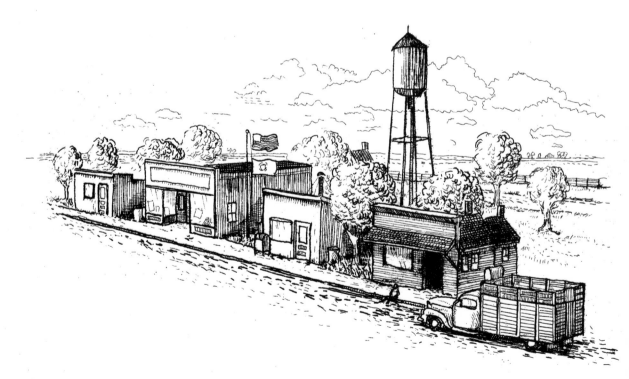